Harry H. Marks

Small Change, or, Lights and Shades of New York

Harry H. Marks

Small Change, or, Lights and Shades of New York

ISBN/EAN: 9783337114183

Printed in Europe, USA, Canada, Australia, Japan

Cover: Foto ©Andreas Hilbeck / pixelio.de

More available books at **www.hansebooks.com**

SMALL CHANGE;

OR,

LIGHTS AND SHADES OF NEW YORK.

BY

HARRY H. MARKS.

———◆———

NEW YORK:

THE STANDARD PUBLISHING COMPANY,

NO. 30 VESEY STREET.

1882.

PUBLISHER'S PREFACE.

The sketches published in this volumne depict some of the most interesting phases of life in New York, as seen by a newspaper reporter. Several have appeared in the columns of the *N. Y. World*, the *Chicago Times*, the *Illustrated Weekly* and other journals with which the author was formerly connected. They are now presented to the public for the first time in book form, the publishers believing that they are worthy of more enduring favor than usually attaches to newspaper articles.

The names of the people who figured in the incidents reported have, for obvious reasons, been suppressed or altered and, in some instances, the author has slightly modified the stiffness of stereotyped newspaper phraseology. With these exceptions, the volume consists literally of leaves from a reporter's note book, and the articles are, for the most part, statements of verified facts, gathered in the course of a ten years experience on the press.

THE STANDARD PUBLISHING CO.

No. 30 VESEY STREET, N. Y.

CONTENTS.

FEW of the millions of readers, who every morning eagerly scan their daily papers in search of the latest news, and praise or blame their editors, according to their feelings, ever give as much as a thought to that hard-worked and much-abused class, the reporters, who, on the previous day, were scouring the country, near and far, in search of choice bits of political scandal or social gossip, which are dished up to the public in such an inviting form. To most of them the reporter is either an unimportant personage, unworthy of their notice, or a monster of iniquity too awful to think of. In fact, he is neither. Once a reporter myself, I claim to know something of my former *confreres;* and, I propose to tell it.

The American newspaper reporters are no longer mere machines for reporting speeches or chronicling the dry details of daily occurrences, like their counterparts in the old-fashioned journalism of Europe. Their duties are various and important; and, by their faithful performance of them, they have contributed largely toward earning for the journals of this country the high reputation that they enjoy at home and abroad. The biographers and eulogists of other men, they have no one to sound their praise unless they do it themselves. Their work being altogether anonymous, they get no credit for it outside of the offices in which they work, and their only recompense is their professional pay, which is shamefully inadequate.

Newspaper reporters may be divided into two classes—viz: the short-hand reporters, whose duties are chiefly mechanical, and who report trials, speeches, sermons, etc., and the news reporters who write descriptive articles, serious and humorous, describe processions, balls, and other gatherings, and report political and social sensations, tragic or romantic, and compose local articles of the lighter order, The members of both classes must be men of good education and pleasant address. The latter, moreover, must have a facility for rapid, easy, and graceful writing, as well as a good general knowledge of men and things. As a rule, reporters are young men between the ages of 18 and 30. Frequently they are men of university training and good social position, who enter a newspaper office with the pay of a stage-driver, in the usually vain hope of working their way up to an editorial position. This they very rarely do, however, for the reason that if a man is a good reporter his services in that line are too valuable to be dispensed with; and if he is not a good reporter, he does not stay long enough on any one paper to earn promotion. The vast majority of the men, entering at an early age upon a precarious and Bohemian sort of existence, are soon disheartened at their poor prospects; and, if their position is such as to oblige them to remain at the work, they become dissipated and lose all ambition to rise to a higher place. Many a reporter, who had begun life at 20, with fair hopes of a brilliant future, has found himself at middle age no better off than when he began. This, partly because the better positions are very few, and partly|because promotion goes more often by favor than by merit.

A young man leaving college at 18, who goes into a newspaper office, to begin life as a reporter, without influence either with the editor or in the publisher's department, is put at police court work at $12 or $15 a week. His hours are from 9 or 10 A. M. until midnight, and his work is of the most tiresome and monotonous character. After a year or so he may be promoted to office reporting at $25, or at the outside $35 a week; and he is obliged to report for assignment daily at 11 A. M. and 5 P. M., so that he may be called upon at any time to engage in work that will keep him up half the night. He may be in this position for years, with no prospect of bettering himself, unless he has influence or uncommon luck, until he hies him to the country to take charge of some country sheet of which he *may* ultimately become the proprietor. Usually, however, he continues in town, adding to his income by corresponding for provincial papers and eking out a living as best he may. Sometimes his wide acquaintance with all kinds of men may get him a small political position or a place in some corporation; but this happens very seldom.

The experienced reporter, who knows the ins and outs of the offices, always prefers "working on space"—that is being paid by the article—to receiving a salary. The reason for this is clear. If he has a salary of $35, he may have to write ten columns a week, and still he gets no extra pay. But, if he works on space, he gets from $5 to $10 a column, and is paid according to what he does; making sometimes $50 or $60 a week. Besides, he has the advantage of being able to work just when he chooses, and may write

for as many papers as he likes. Nevertheless, "the space man" is
not entirely happy. If he is sent to report some big event and
writes two columns, he is liable, in the event of there being a
crush of news, to have his article cut down three-fourths; and, in
most offices, he is then paid only for what is printed instead of
for what he wrote. This is a constant annoyance to him. Often
his best stories are cruelly mutilated; what promised to be a good
day's work is reduced to a paltry job; and the persons from whom
he got his information accuse him of garbling their statements
and misrepresenting them. Nor do his troubles end here. If he
is not on good terms with the city editor or his assistants, his
stories may be continually cut without reason, or assignments
may be with-held from him. Most of all, in some offices, if he is
sent to attend to a certain matter, and, after ten or twelve hours
work, gets only ten lines, he is paid for these ten lines only, and
receives no consideration for his time. He may have spent a
dollar or two in car fare; but according to the rules in some offices
he can only charge for expenses out of town; so that if, in this
given case, he has not had to leave the city, he is actually a loser
by the day's work. Among other injustices he suffers is this; he
is ordered to write a special article, and devotes two or three days
to the work, taking no other assignments in the meanwhile. His
article completed, he hands it to the city editor, who sometimes
delays its publication, for one reason or another, for several weeks,
during which time the reporter has to wait for his money; for
nothing is paid for until it is published. Of course, at the end of
the week in which he wrote the article, his bill is very small; and,
equally, of course, he is too impecunious not to feel the effects of
having to wait two or three weeks for his pay.

Naturally, the reader will ask: But why do the reporters stand
such treatment? The answer is simply that they cannot help
themselves. They are usually poor men. They have no trades
union or protective association. If they resign, there are hundreds of others to take their places; for there are always a
number of men of good education anxious to get work enough to
keep body and soul together. And so they prefer to accept a half
a loaf to having to go without bread. But do the editors allow
such impositions? Well, with a few bright exceptions, yes. The
chief editors come little in contact with the reporters; and, as for
the managing editors, for the most part they are too anxious to
curry favor with the publishers by the practice of rigid economy(!)
to allow the question of fairness or justice to enter into their con-
siderations. To the publishers, as a rule, he is the best managing

editor who has the smallest bills. And the managing editors know this. Their own positions are not secure enough for them to afford to ignore it, and so the unfortunate reporters suffer.

Apart from the pecuniary difficulties of reporters, there are others almost unknown outside of the profession. It frequently happens that the editors, in their anxiety to "beat" one another in obtaining the earliest news, resort to the most undignified and disagreeable means to get such information as they want, and the reporters, of course, are the tools they employ. To the credit of my *confreres*, be it said, that I have personally known of many instances of reporters refusing point blank to accept assignments which would compromise them as gentlemen. During the Beecher trial, some of the papers were in the habit of sending reporters to wait on the doorsteps of prominent people concerned in that famous scandal, to spy upon their actions, and to report who went in and out of doors. They had to choose their men, though; for many a reporter, poor though he might be, would not stoop to such work. Fancy the position of a reporter who is sent to interview the widow of some murdered man, while the bleeding corpse of her husband lies in an adjoining room! Think of the pleasant task assigned another of going to see Mr. Brown, on the evening of the day on which his wife died, to inquire whether she left a will! I know of an instance of a reporter being sent to interview a young lady whose affianced husband had just committed suicide. The lady had not heard the news, and the reporter was the first to break it to her. She swooned, and he, perhaps ashamed of his position, left in haste, probably to be scolded by the city editor for not waiting until she recovered and interviewing her then. It is a common practice, when a prominent person dies and the papers have no material for an obituary, to send a reporter at once to the house to interview the surviving widow or orphans in regard to the life of the deceased. Sometimes, I am glad to say, the relatives kick the reporter downstairs, but, sometimes they are so overcome with grief that they have not the spirit to resent the insolent intrusion. In such cases as these, however, a reporter, who is at the same time a gentleman, will either respectfully decline the assignment, or take it and fulfill it in his own way and in a respectable manner. I do not think that any reporter is obliged at any time to compromise himself by undertaking a distasteful duty like this; but it is certainly not the fault of the editors if the reporters are not, all of them, a pack of sneaking, keyhole detectives.

My own experience, extending over seven years, is that a gentleman can be a reporter, and still be a gentleman. But it is difficult. The reporter who has not to reproach himself with having ever abused his position to obtrude upon the privacy of grief, to insult the defenceless or to act the spy, must have had a hard road to travel. He is, perhaps, an exceptional member of his class. I hope he may not remain so. There are blacklegs in all the walks of life; and ours is no exception to the rule. Let the dirty work of the press be done by them. Let the respectable members of the profession stand aloof from area-sneaking and death-bed interviewing. And let the public remember that there are reporters— and reporters.

A DOSE OF MORPHINE.

WHEN I was a lad I served a term as clerk in a drug store down South, where, when I was not occupied in putting up two-ounce vials of castor oil, or in ladling out colocynth apples or cayenne, I used to find much pleasure in poring over De Quincey's Recollections of an Opium Eater That work had a remarkable effect upon me. It gave birth to a craving for opium, which was bound to be satisfied sooner or later. It happened to be sooner. Availing myself one day of the run of the establishment which I enjoyed, I succeeded in getting a box of opium pills, which¶to my mind, contained the material wherewith to manufacture all the joys of which De Quincey had so eloquently discoursed.

With the pills in my pocket, I hied me home, and, on a glorious sunny Sunday afternoon, I divested myself of my outer garments, pulled down the blinds, lighted a couple of pastilles, put De Quincey on a chair by my bedside, and—swallowed three pills. I lay down and waited for the bliss to come. The pills worked, but the bliss did not come worth a cent. But a splitting headache did and after that a feeling of nausea almost indescribable, and in thirty minutes I was as sick as the proverbial dog. I threw up— all my theories of opium and opium eating; I flung De Quincey out of the window, and I went to bed a less experimental but more experienced youth. This happened some ten years ago, and from that time to this I have had a holy horror of opium in any form.

A week ago I went to a celebrated and most incompetent dentist to have a tooth extracted. In extracting it, the dentist did—what many men had threatened to do before him,-but never actually did—he broke my jaw. That is, he splintered it and put me in more pain than I remember ever to have endured before. The splintered bones had to be cut out, of course, and that did not make me much the happier. At last, in desperate agony, I went to my friend, Dr. Kenneth Reid, for relief, and he gave me a hypodermic injection of morphine. That did help me—for a time. Did you ever have a hypodermic injection of morphine? Well do; it is just too funny for any thing. At first you only feel a little annoyed at your doctor for sticking a needle in your arm to no purpose. Next you experience a cramp in your head and a buzzing in your ear. Then the pain goes away, and you feel like a Tammany ratification meeting and don't know your heels from a band of music. At last you go to sleep and dream, dream the whole encyclopædia, the dictionary, the gazeteer, your family history, the family history of all your friends and the Patent office reports for twenty years back. You feel your brain travelling straight ahead at the rate of a thousand miles a minute. You are distinctly sensible of your brain knocking up against your cranium in its hurry to overtake what has gone before it. Finally you wake up in a firing perspiration and your tongue hanging out of your mouth, your eyeballs way down on your cheek, and a general feeling of physical bankruptcy. But the pain has gone, and a glass of vichy or two, a warm bath and a cigar soon set you right, and you come to the conclusion, that I have reached, that opium properly and timely used, is a good thing, after all.

PRIVATE DETECTIVES.

AMERICAN life is modelled after that of France much more closely than we are generally willing to admit. This is true of our dress, our food, our theatres, our literature, and notably of our system of espionage, known as the private detective service. Born of the mutual fears and suspicions engendered among the nobles of France during the revolutionary periods, fostered under the rule of the Napoleonic dynasty, and spreading with time and political complications throughout Europe, this institution was transplanted to America quite recently, and has grown slowly and by stealth. The war did much to develope it, our elaborate and complicated revenue system needs its aid, and the demoralized condition of society since the war has given it countenance and support.

There is something in the very name of "private detective" which is repulsive to the frank and honest mind; its very sound arouses curiosity, and, one might almost say suspicion. Nevertheless, detectives are a very necessary element of any well-ordered society, and, if their services were directed exclusively towards the ferreting out of crime, they would, no doubt, have the unreserved support of the community. But unfortunately the power they wield is, by some of them, used as often for evil as for good. The system under which they work is so lose and so dangerous that it virtually gives the reputations of the whole community into the keeping of a totally irresponsible and frequently untrustworthy class.

The private, or, as it might be called, the amateur detective service of New York, is conducted on veritable *laisser faire* principles. It has no such restrictions as are imposed upon the "private inquiry offices" in London, or the "bureaux d'information" in Paris. Any one is free to engage in it, and to make all he can out of it. It is often the refuge of dishonest and incompetent men who have been discharged from the police service, and who, with their wealth of experience and poverty of principle, are enabled to filch a good living by it. It is the last resort of broken-down lawyers, and of the "rag-tail and bobtail" of the professional classes. It is the favorite vocation of that not inconsiderable class of people who find their chief pleasure in minding their neighbor's business. But it includes also many very estimable men, adapted by nature and training for the discharge of their delicate duties; and although New York may have more than her quota of bungling and incompetent detectives, she has quite as many good officers as she needs.

Most of the private detective work is done through the medium of the so called detective agencies. These establishments, of which there are about fifty in New York, are managed by men belonging to the various classes just described and, as a rule, they pay profitably. The "bosses" employ green hands at salaries ranging from $7 to $15 a week, and charge their patrons from $7 to $10 a day, per man; so that it is to the interest of both "boss" and employee to work as slowly as possible. The result is that delicate work is often intrusted to incompetant hands, and sadly bungled; that arbitrary arrests are often made, and, worst of all, that many of the under-paid "officers" are in a position to make money illegitimately—and they are seldom of the class to resist the temptation. A year or so ago, an officer was sent to arrest an absconding clerk, who had stolen $10,000 of his employer's money. Though the fugitive did not leave the country, he was never arrested, and the officer never returned. It sometimes happens, too, that these detectives, when employed in civil cases, sell their services to both sides. The character of these men is so well known that their evidence in a court of justice is frequently discredited, in which cases the money paid them is simply thrown away.

One of the most glaring instances of detective rascality the writer has ever known is that of a United States Secret Service employee, who was engaged some years ago in ferreting out some custom-house frauds in this city. In the discharge of his duty, he gained access to the books and correspondence of a large importing firm, and, among the letters that came into his possession, were several involving the reputation of a married lady of good social standing. He made known his discovery to the husband of the lady in question, and by threats of exposure succeeded in extorting large sums of money. He continued his black-mailing for years, and finally sold the letters he had stolen for a good round sum, on which he has lived ever since. You may see this fellow nearly every day; his face is familiar to all New Yorkers, and yet, such is the power he has over the welfare and reputation of two families, that no one dares denounce him.

But let us glance for a moment at a pleasanter phase of our subject, the clever detection of frauds by competent and honest officers. A few months ago, William Biffi, formerly of the Paris Secret Service, and detective of the late Assembly Commitee on Crime, was engaged by a large piano-firm, in New York to get evidence for the prosecution of a manufacturer of "bogus" pianos. To accomplish his difficult task, Biffi went into regular partnership with the "bogus" firm, mastered all the details of the trade, and, when the case came to trial, appeared against his partners as a witness for the prosecution. The result was, of course, perfectly successful. Another very clever detective is Taggart, Col. Tom Scott's special man, who has recently been elected State Senator in Pennsylvania.

Among the many purposes for which private detectives are employed are those of hunting up missing men, women and children, securing evidence in divorce cases, watching and protecting banks and other public institutions, "spotting" fraudulent creditors and suspicious characters generally, and "keeping an eye" on fast young men and family "black sheep." Every bank and every hotel in the city has its own private detective, who watches all who come and all who go, from the partners and officers to the bell-boys and messengers. It is told of the president of a well known banking institution, that, now and again, he sends for some one of his clerks and holds some such conversation as this:

"Last Tuesday," he will say, "you spent the evening in Jones' billiard saloon, did you not?"

"Yes, sir," will stammer the astonished clerk.

"You took, during the evening, six rounds of drinks with your three companions, of which you paid for four, did you not?"

"Yes, sir," replies the astonished youth.

"Then you went to Mills" and lost $15 at faro, is it not so? Don't deny it—I know. I know all about you.

The President will then go on and tell his man where he lives, how he lives, whom he associates with, and where he gets his clothes; all this to let him see he is watched, and to warn him against wrong doing of any kind.

Without discussing the wisdom of subjecting a man to such a system of surveillance as this, without defending the man who has so little self-respect as to submit to it, it must be said that it is very effective in keeping young men in the right path.

Private detectives are frequently employed by stock speculators on Wall Street, and it is well known that one prominent broker has two of the smartest men in the country in his pay. It is related that, a few months ago, a large operator on "the street" employed a detective to watch his partner, whom he suspected of playing him false. The same officer was, within a few days, engaged by the gentleman whom he was watching, to pay similar attention to his suspicious partner, whom *he* suspected of playing him false. When business is dull, the private detective sometimes degenerates into a city guide, and employs his time in showing the unsophisticated countryman the metropolitan elephant. Other pleasant and light occupations are those of "shadowing" young ladies of good social position, suspected of associating with unworthy characters, by no means a rare occurence; or "piping," or tracking husbands who go off on suspicious "excursions," and stay out late at their "clubs." These are the social features of the detective business, and they have been brought pretty near to perfection.

A knowledge of several languages is a great advantage, and the ability to move in various circles of society is almost a necessity for a successful detective. To these qualifications should be added a specia. .ove of detective occupation. This is a common merit with women, many of whom are employed as "divorce detectives," and who, perhaps. by reason of the natural inquisitiveness and officiousness of their sex, seem to bring to their work more enthusiasm and not less success than their male rivals.

THE SOCIETY THIEF.

THE recent exposure of an eminently respectable society-gentleman who, for years past has made a practice of attending fashionable balls and receptions for the purpose of stealing whatever articles of value he could lay his hands on, carries with it a very interesting and instructive moral. It is hardly probable that he represents any considerable number of society thieves, but the ease with which he gained the *entree* to fashionable and wealthy circles suggests the idea that if he has not had, or does not have, many imitators it will not be for the lack of opportunity afforded to would-be plunderers to follow his example. This particular thief appears to be a man of good family connections, of fair education, and of uncommon natural ability. He has been possessed of some means, quite sufficient to enable him to live decently well, but his ambition was to shine in society, to be foremost in the brilliant gatherings of the *beau monde*, to dress well, to live like a wealthy man—and this he could not do without a considerably larger income than he had. This ambition, frequently indulged, in part at least, and there being but one obstacle in the way of its permanent achievement, viz: his impecuniosity, it became with him a perfect mania and he determined to indulge himself, at the expense of society and at the sacrifice of all moral principle.

Unfortunately, American society is not at all particular as to a man's business occupation, as long as he is well-dressed and seems to have plenty of money he may come and go as he pleases and "no questions asked." The society thief knew this and, knowing, took advantage of it, to plunder his acquaintances of "the upper ten" in order to get the means to vie with them in fashionable extravagances. How many other men have done the same thing on a smaller scale? And who is more to blame for the possibility of such acts than that very society which, in the present instance, is the chief victim?

As long as wealth is the one key to so-called good society, unprincipled men will be found willing and ready to secure that key as best they may; honestly if they can, dishonestly if they must. If the conditions of a good standing in society were more exacting and dependent upon other, and worthier, qualifications than that of wealth, the case would be different, and there would be less unscrupulous scrambling for social advancement. It is all very well to prate about the danger of caste-distinctions in American society; it is very pretty to brag about the glorious equality of all men in our country and in our time, but the results are dangerous in the extreme, and one of them is just this; that it serves to encourage such dishonesty as the society thief is guilty of.

The very curse of American life is the one constant scramble among all classes to be better and higher than they are. The dry goods clerk wants to live like his employer, and steals, that he may be enabled to do so; the government clerk wants a higher government position, and steals, that he may buy it; the Alderman wants to go to Congress, and steals, to buy votes; the Congressman wants to be a Senator, and steals that he may buy the legislatures; and so it goes on through our whole national and social life. No one is satisfied, every one wants to rise higher than he is, and the powerful motive for all is money—money which must be had in some way or the other. If the petty clerk understood, once for all, that merit, and merit alone, would bring him social and business advancement; if the politician knew absolutely that no amount of money would secure him social or political preferment, unless his money were backed by real worth; if, in short, we would dethrone the cursed dollar, and re-enthrone moral principle, society thieves might soon cease to exist. Until that time comes, if it ever does, people will go on stealing, that they may steal enough to secure immunity from punishment. For, unfortunately, the effect of our whole political life, and, especially, of the recent compromises with the thieves of political rings, is to teach that stealing is no crime, so long as one steals enough to pay for the law's delays, or to compromise with his victims.

SOME CONFIDENCE GAMES..

DETECTIVES who detect are not, as a rule, a very talkative class of men, but when they do talk they have usually something of interest to relate. This is the case with one of the oldest and most experienced men in the business, who, in conversation with the writer, a few days ago, explained a few of the many swindling games played upon greenhorns, coming to New York from the country, by professional sharpers and confidence men. These are numerous and varied, and, as there is no law against them, specifically, they can only be punished when they are successful, and when their perpetrators can be held on the charge of actually obtaining money under false pretences.

One of the oldest and simplest frauds of this class is carried on chiefly upon the wharves and in the streets around the river. It is performed thus: A, a confidence man ,scrapes an acquaintance with some simple-looking countryman, who has a promising air, and gets into conversation with him. After plying him with drink and finding out something about the state of his finances, he tells him that he is about to take a dozen valuable race-horses to California, and is seeking a man to help him attend to them on the journey. The countryman offers his services, and is engaged at a liberal salary and the two start to see the horses. On their way, they are met by B, the confederate, who angrily demands immediate payment of a livery and feed bill which he has against A. A looks in his pocket-book, is surprised to find that he has no cash with him and offers B a check, which B refuses to take. A, then, prevails upon the countryman to cash the check or to lend him the required amount until he can go to the bank; disappearance of A and B; discomfiture of O.

Another ingenious swindle is known to the police as "the belt game" and is played thus: Some wealthy and green old farmer, generally a German, comes to New York, with a large sum of money, *en route* to Europe,to visit his family or friends. He wanders,or is decoyed, into the office of a swindling exchange broker, who offers to sell him English or German gold for American greenbacks at a very small commission. The farmer, usually suspicious, asks to see the money and is, accordingly shown and has counted out to him the genuine coin; but, as he is about to leave, the "broker" warns him that it is not safe to carry so much money about with him and, by working upon his fears, persuades him that he ought to get a belt. Strangely enough it happens that the "broker" has got a belt, that he can sell him, and into it the farmer puts the money himself. When he has finished his task, he is asked into the back-office to undress and put it on and, while he is undressing, the original belt is dexterously changed for one just like it but containing nickel coins instead of the real gold. Then the "broker," solicitous for the welfare of his victim whose entire confidence he has gained by this time, accompanies him to the dock and sees him safely on board his ship. Even when this precaution is not taken, the victim is usually too careful of his money to take it from his body and examine it until he is on board.

The trick recently sought to be played upon Mr. Shillaber is well known and almost "played out." Swindler No. 1 approaches a countryman on the streets and grasping him by the hand, exclaims, "Why my dear Mr Smith, how do you do? When did you come from Racine?" The man thus accosted in nine cases out of ten sees through the trick, but in the tenth case he will reply, smiling, "Why my name ain't Smith, stranger, nor I don't come from Racine, I am Jones of Peoria!" Swindler No. 1 apologizes, of course, and goes away to his accomplice and, to use the police-phrase, "gives him the steer." Swindler No. 2 now follows Jones all day and, towards evening or, it may be, next day approaches him with; "Hallo, Jones, how are you? Ain't seen you since I was down to Peoria last year. How's the folks?" Jones does not know the man, shows it by his looks, when, the swindler, reading his thoughts, adds: "Guess you hardly remember me, shaved my whiskers off since I met you there at the hotel." Now Jones feels more easy, he has been having a few drinks and is afraid his memory may be bad; any way he allows his new acquaintance to show him around, takes a few more drinks and, before the day is over, he has either cashed a check taken a lottery ticket or had his pocket picked.

A very simple and frequently successful dodge, played chiefly by the youthful sharper, was next described by the detective as follows: a well-dressed man walking along the streets, usually at night, is accosted by a small boy who, in a mysterious manner says to him, holding a ring, "say, mister, here's a ring wot I found; looks like gold; won't yer buy it? I don't want it." Usually the cupidity of the man is excited and, thinking the boy does not know the value of the trinket, which has initials engraved on it, he looks around to see that the coast is clear and, giving the youth a couple of dollars, hurries off with his prize. He is afraid to look at his purchase until he gets home and then he examines it, perhaps tests it, and invariably finds that a dollar a gross will buy him as many more such rings as he may have occasion for.

The sawdust-swindle, which has been frequently exposed, is one of the oldest of its kind and used to pay well; but it is going out of practice of late. It was generally conducted by a firm, having an office in some respectable part of town. which entered into correspondence with young men all over the country, offering to sell them counterfeit money at about the rate of $10 for $1. The parties so addressed would send on the money and receive a box of sawdust or the sawdust would be sent C. O. D. and paid for before the box was opened. Another trick of the same sort and one which is constantly played is that of bogus watches. This is monopolized by one or two large firms in this city, one of which at least has made a fortune by it and is well-known and closely watched by the police, but without much effect. The bogus-watch firm writes to people in various parts of the country, on regular business paper and in regular business style, informing them that their gold watches, left for repairs, are now ready and that if the amount of the bill, usually $10, is paid they will be sent by express and otherwise they will be sold to pay expenses. The parties so addressed, think there is some mistake, fondly imagine that there is a chance of getting a gold watch for $10 and s nd on the money. They either receive in return a brass watch worth about $2 or, as is sometimes the case, they never hear anything more about it. Of the same class of tricks, are those of advertising: "a fine sewing machine for $10" and then sending on a small instrument worth $2. A large number of the so-called Spiritualist mediums advertisements are of this class. The spiritualist papers are full of advertisements of "lady mediums" and others offering to answer letters from Spirit-land, to tell the past and forecast the future for fees ranging from 50 cents to $2 per message. Needless to say they are traps set to catch fools.

Among the commonest street-swindlers are; the Mephistophelian foreigner who approaches you with an offer to sell smuggled silk or laces or cigars "dirt-cheap;' the man who finds a pocket book full of money and insists that you dropped it and will take a moderate reward for its return and vanishes before you discover that the contents are counterfeit ; the old lady who has lost her pocket-book and wants to borrow twenty-five cents to get home to Brooklyn; the small boy who has had "all my papers stolen, boss, by a big boy" and wants twenty-five cents to get more; the woman who has just "been discharged from the

Treasury department" and wants money to get a lodging;" these, and others too numerous to mention, swell the long-list of professional swindlers who prey upon the unsophisticated countryman and the credulous city man. The mole fraud is particularly versatile, when business is slack he will pick pockets, "steer" for gambling houses, beg or burglarize,—he is not particular. Usually he is too clever for the police and hence his usual immunity from punishment.

GIFTS TO THE BRIDE.

THE following advertisement has appeared daily for months in one of the New York papers, and was upon its first appearance hailed as a bit of irony:

DUPLICATE WEDDING PRESENTS
BOUGHT OR EXCHANGED.
Address J. H. JOHNSTON, Jeweller, 150 Bowery.

It is a genuine business advertisement, however. The writer called upon Mr. Johnston last week at his store and found him willing to talk. A jeweller by trade, Mr. Johnston is a man of many resources and one who prides himself upon his knowledge of human nature. He is, moreover, a man of good education, and entertained Walt Whitman a. his house when he was in the city. In answer to the reporter's inquiries Mr. Johnston said that the jewelry business is dull just now, but the traffic in "duplicate wedding presents" is particularly lively. He receives numerous answers to his advertisement, some of them from people well known in society; he visits them at their houses, appraises their goods and buys them, if they wish to sell.

"What do you pay for goods and how?" asked the writer.

"For silverware," was the reply, "I pay by the ounce, say from $1 to $3 an ounce. For jewelry I pay what I consider a fair market price, according to the value of the articles. What do I do with my purchases? Why, I sell them again, either to the customers of my store or to dealers at a small advance on the purchase price, and always for less than they could possibly be bought for in the regular way. Here, for example, is a fine silver kettle I bought at half its actual value and put it in the window. Yesterday one of the firm that made it called in and offered to buy it at my own price. He said he did not want it "kicking around town" with his mark on it. Here is a lot of silver which recently figured among the presents at a fashionable wedding. In cost $350, and weighs 150 ounces. I paid $300 for it, and I will sell it for $350. And here is a solid silver tea set that cost $900, and I can sell it for $400 and make a good profit."

"What class of people sell their wedding presents?"

"All classes, especially in these times.. Money is too valuable to be locked up in useless silver kettles and urns that you have to pay for keeping in a safe deposit company. Whenever I read of a stylish wedding somewhere, I look at the list of presents, and I know that I shall have a customer before long. They all claim to sell only duplicate presents, of course. It is none of my business to ask where the duplicates are. I buy whatever I can sell at a profit, *voila tout*. Of course, my business is confidential; I am as silent as the tomb. I have to be, for mutual confidence is an essential of the business."

A recent purchase of Mr. Johnston's is a beautiful pearl neck lace which, he says, recently adorned the neck of a bride whose marriage was a society sensation; another is a pair of bracelets valued in the market at $1,200, and still another is an 8-carat diamond, for which he asks $7,000. "You have no idea of the extent of this business," said he, showing these articles: "why, there are families in this city who have been living ever since the panic of 1873 upon their plate and jewelry, and keeping up appearances, too. See that solid silver pitcher; that was presented years ago to a well-known gentleman by A. T. Stewart, Wm. B. Astor, Brown Brothers and others. He died some time ago and the pitcher passed into the hands of some relatives or friends who got hard-up, and here it is. I will sell it for $250. There on the side were the names of Stewart and Astor. I erased, them, and if you want to present it to Mayor Grace, I will engrave his name on it and give it to you cheap."

"How long has the traffic in wedding presents been going on?"

"Not more than five or six years. It is more general now than ever. Money is in demand; plate and paste take the place of silver and diamonds; nobody is any the wiser and several people are so much the richer. This is a practical age, and this business grows out of its practicality."

GRINDERS OF THE ORGAN.

THERE are about 300 organ-grinders in New York City. They are mostly Italians, about 90 per cent of them coming from the sunny South, the other 10 per cent being made up of Germans, Frenchmen and one-legged ex-American soldiers. They pay no license for the privilege of pursuing their painful profession and, judging from the police records, which show that only ten were arrested last year, they are, except when operating upon their instruments of torture, peaceably disposed people. The Italian organ-grinder is usually an ex-peasant farmer who, failing in business, or infringing some law in his own land, comes to America relying upon the reputation of his countrymen for musical talent to make a living. He is usually rather short of money, and frequently has to borrow the means to buy his instrument. Rarely he tramps over the Alps, and landing in Paris buys his organ there for much less than it would cost here, and brings it with him. If he comes here without an organ, he can get one only by paying cash for it, as one man has a monopoly of the business, and transacts it on C. O. D. terms. This man is Mr. Taylor, of Chatham square and New Bowery, who has the only street organ factory on this continent, and one of three which are known in the world. The other two are those of Eimhoff & Co., of London, whose instruments are manufactured at the village of Volkirk, in the Black Forest, and of Gaviole & Co., of Paris, who make their own organs. These three houses make all the instruments in use, and renew each other's goods as frequently as they need renewing.

The hand organ is certainly of ancient origin. It is an imitation of the church organ, whose invention is attributed to Archimedes about 220 B. C., and which was first brought to Europe from the Greek empire and applied to religious uses in churches A. D. 657. The hand-organ is constructed mainly on the same principle, but on a smaller scale. A bellows within the instrument is worked by turning a winch, and, by the same action, by means of an endless screw, a cylinder or drum is turned. On this cylinder the tunes are set in brass pins or staples, at the distances required by the lengths and successions of the notes, just as on the cylinder of a musical box. The pins raise keys, which press down stickers and open valves, admitting air to the pipes used. Each instrument has an average of about ten tunes. When the performer has played enough of one tune, he pulls a stop which shifts the cylinder and puts the brass pins in position to play upon the keys

of the music in the next tune.   Mr. Taylor explained the simple
process by which this is done, and said he can change one or two
tunes at a time by simply taking out the pins and replacing them
by new ones, or, if several new tunes are needed, he puts in a new
cylinder.   Composers and music publishers frequently send him
their latest tunes, with requests that he will put them on his organs;
but he selects only such as are popular or are likely to become so.
His sales average over one hundred organs a year, and he sometimes turns out three or four a week.   These vary in price from
$100 to $200 for a common street organ, to which extra cylinders
of nine tunes each can be added at a cost of $35.   The side-show
organs, with forty-two keys, four stop-pipes, nine tunes with cym-
bals, bells, castanets and trumpets, and the automaton brass band
with sixty keys, four stop-pipes, thirty-five brass trumpets, large
and small drums, triangles and nine tunes, which are seen rarely
in the streets, but frequently at cheap shows, cost all the way
from $500 to $2,000 each.

Mr. Taylor sends organs all over the Continent and has a large
number of customers in South America and Cuba.   When any
one orders an organ he selects his own tunes, the manufacturer
gets the music and transfers the notes to the cylinder of the organ
by means of the brass pins alluded to.   A large part of the business consists of changing tunes.   The South American organ
grinder changes most frequently, as he has to vary his repertoire
with every revolution.   He sends to Mr. Taylor the piano-forte
accompaniment of some revolutionary air or Spanish fandango, and
receives his organ shortly after metamorphosed into a new instrument.   Just before St. Patrick's Day Mr. Taylor had calls from
numerous gentlemen of the organ grinding profession and there
was a great demand for "Wearing of the Green." "St. Patrick's
Day Parade" and "Killarney's Lakes."   When an organ-grinder,
for some reason or another, selects a route which is inhabitated
largely by people of one nationality he changes the tune on his
instrument to suit their tastes.   Thus if he goes into a German
quarter he takes the "Wacht am Rhein" with him, if to a French
quarter the "Marseillaise," if to an Irish quarter he selects the
lively airs of Erin.   The organ grinder is nothing if not cosmopolitan; he is not committed to the music of the past, present or
future, and takes to the airs of Strauss, Offenbach, Verdi or Men-
delssohn with a philosophical equanimity and a truly artistic
impartiality.   It must be added, however, that he plays them all
with equal ease.

The organ business is conducted on a cash basis.   The grinder gets ready money and pays ready money. Mr. Taylor says the only time he ever lost any money was just after the close of the war, when a number of one-legged and one-armed soldiers were ambitious to embark upon an organ-grinding career. They had no money, but several gentlemen, full of gratitude for their brave deeds, went security for them. They got their organs, and Mr. Taylor, to use his own words, got "stuck for $4,000"

The barrel-organ, at present in use, has almost completely superseded the old-fashioned hurdy-gurdy or piano-organ, which was a string instrument and only fit to play jigs. The barrel-organ is a pipe instrument and, when in tune, which it generally is not, is not to be despised. The great appolonicon, which made such a sensation in London some years ago, was nothing more than a gigantic barrel-organ. It stood 24 feet high and 30 feet broad. It could be played by three large cylinders, or by six performers on six sets of keys, and was the largest hand-organ ever made.

The organ-grinder's existence is rather precarious. The profits of his calling fluctuate, not only with the state of business but also with the seasons. In wet weather, when there are but few people on the street, he, of course, makes less than in fine weather when he plays to large, though transient, audiences. In the summer, and particulary in the poorer neighborhoods, where the girls being deprived of the pleasures of hotel-hops at the watering places, sometimes get up impromptu Germans on the sidewalks, he does a rattling good business and is occasionally able to lay up a little for the rainy and snowy days of winter. At all seasons of the year the organ-grinder, of all men, battens on the misfortunes of others; for, strange to say among a music-loving people, he is most liberally paid when the payment is conditional upon his going as far away as possible, and he often receives generous and unexpected gifts when he happens, by chance, to get into a street where some one is ill, dead or dying. Most of them average about 50 cents a day at this time of year. They sometimes make a dollar, but not often. In the summer they average from 75 cents to a dollar a day. It costs the organ grinder, according to his own account, 50 cents a day to live, and all he gets over that sum is clear profit. One of the class, who seems to have traveled much told me once in very bad French that he had played four months in Paris before coming here, and preferred New York to the French capital He used to average 40 centimes (about 8 cents) a day there, and he makes about 50 cents a day here. In Paris, he said, he used to get most of his money from the women, who threw it to him from the windows; here he gets most patronage from the men who pass him in the street. He added that the people are not attracted to the windows here by the sound of an organ as they are in Paris. I asked if there was an understanding among the organ-grinders as to the route each should take, and what would be done if two met on the same block. The answer was that no understanding existed among the profession, and that when two of its members come in contact they both play on with all their muscle until the one who plays louder, drives the other one away and remains master of the field.

The organ-grinder who makes the most money is usually the one who goes around with a woman and a few children, who are under-stood to be his. At the end of two or three tunes, the woman, infant in arm, goes into the shops and bar-rooms in the neighbor-hood, and usually manages to scrape together a few coppers, while the other children accost the passers-by, and sometimes with fair results. When an organ-grinder cannot afford the luxury of a wife and some children, he gets the next best thing—a monkey—which he usually buys of one of his countrymen who deal in those animals. The monkey is often so trained that he can beg quite as importunately as a wife or child, and, as he costs less to keep and clothe, he is considered more economical. Besides, he is funny, which a wife and children sometimes are not. When an organ-grinder has neither a wife and children nor a monkey, he some-times has an instrument, the front of which is fitted with dancing puppets, but this is a useless piece of extravagance, as the puppets cannot beg, will not work and do not add materially to the attract-ions of the organ. On the the contrary, they simply bring to-gether around the performer a crowd of dirty little boys and girls who block up the sidewalk, cause the organ-man to swear in his native Italian, and sometimes provoke the policeman to order him to "move on."

So much for the Italian organ-grinder. The one-legged or one armed ex-soldier, in military costume arrayed, who is familiar to all, occupies a little higher rank in the profession. Instead of trudging around and discoursing music with a liberal and undis-criminating hand all over the city, he takes up his position at the corner of some leading thoroughfare where, in time, he becomes known and is constituted a sort of pensioner on all the business men in the neighborhood. This musical ex-follower of Mars often makes a fair income and is looked upon with charitable and patriotic indulgence. Just after the close of the war the military organ grinders were alarmingly numerous in our streets, but they have decreased of late to tolerable proportions. Many of them have their discharges from the army framed and hung in front of their instruments as a sort of guarantee of good faith. Besides the male organ-grinders, there are a number of women in the profession on their own account. The most noteworthy are those who go around town with a very small instrument on a very large truck in one end of which are huddled two or three children of tender years who usually do the vocal part of the performance by howling lustily while their ostensible mother grinds the instrument. This little family group is generally completed by a poor, sickly little girl, a few years older than the babies in the truck, who goes round with a tin cup soliciting alms. This is, perhaps, the best paying branch of the business.

Last come the poor old women who are seen nightly on Broadway as the theatres are closing, just seen by the light of a dim candle feebly burning on the organ, grinding away at a small and peculiar looking box which emits faint sounds as of a half-smothered infant appealing for help. One of this class is also found every afternoon on Twenty-third street, near the Fifth Avenue Hotel, with an instrument whose chief recommendation is that it cannot be heard. Where it was made, when or by whom, no man knoweth; it might, judging from its age and size, have served as a model for the original article said to have been made by Archimedes 2,000 years ago.

HUMORS OF THE STREETS.

IF, as some carping critics contend, American humor consists, mainly in bad spelling and grotesque exaggerations, then the sign-boards of the metropolis are truly humorous. That the humor is frequently unintentional does not at all detract from its power to amuse, as may be seen from a few specimens of street signs given below.

A Fourth Avenue confectioner has a sign in his shop-window which reads "Pies Open All Night"; an undertaker in the same thoroughfare advertises "everything requisite for a first-class funeral"; a Bowery placard reads, "Home-Made Dining Rooms, Family Oysters"; a West Broadway restaurateur sells "Home-Made Pies, Pastry and Oysters"; a Third Avenue "dive" offers for sale "Coffee and Cakes off the Griddle," and an East Broadway caterer retails "Fresh Salt Oysters" and "Larger Beer." A Fulton Street tobacconist calls himself a "Speculator in Smoke," and a purveyor of summer drinks has invented a new draught which he calls by the colicky name of "Eolian Spray." A Sixth Avenue barber hangs out a sign reading "Boots Polished Inside," and on Varick Street, near Carmine, there are "Lessons given on the Piano with use for Practice." Cloth Cuttt and Bastd" is the cabalistic legend on the front of a millinery shop on Spring Street.

A mender of old umbrellas has a sign-board reading: "This is the celebrated umbrella hospital, where broken bones are set without pain or use of chloroform. No incurable cases sent out! Invalids called for and sent home sound." A Broadway dealer in "Gents' Furnishing Goods" sells "Patent Irrepressible Shirts," and a Brooklyn dealer in head-covering calls himself a "a practical and classical hatter." A Fourth Avenue hosier deals in "perfect gentlemen's outfits." An East Broadway livery stable is described by its proprietor as "Hotel de Horse." "Crosbie's Country Pork established 1859," is sold on Ninth Avenue, and "Ladies' lunch with polite attendants" is to be had at a moderate price on Fourteenth Street. On South Fifth Avenue is a sign which reads "washing whitewashing and going out to days' work done in the back room," and on Centre Street is a sign-board bearing the inscriptions, "Calsoming & Wall Coloring, Boilers. Grates, & Furnesses Set, Ovens Built, Sewers and Drains put in Curbs, Gutters, and Repairing. All branches attended to." A Chatham Street shirt store is known as "Society for the Encouragement of Wearing Clean Shirts," and a sign on Fiftieth Street near Ninth Avenue reads, "kindling wood yard furniture removed with care." A Brooklyn express wagon, apparently owned by a disciple of Josh Billings, has this inscription, "Orl Kines of horling Dun." "Fancy Goods, Law blanks and fishing tackle" are sold at a store in Hoboken. "Mrs. Captain McCoy, teacher of practical navigation," resides on Madison Street.

It is strange how oddly names contrast sometimes, and sometime agree with the vocations of their owners, thus Ig. Weinbear keeps a wine and beer saloon as do also Messrs. Kaltwasser & Co. Bearup & Carraher is the name of a shipping firm, and the Misses Hooper deal in hoopskirts. Sartorius is a tailor on Third Avenue. Jacob Ables brews, and Peter Ahles sells beer. Butcher & Butler are in the plumbing business. Mr. Carman is a driver, and Mr. Carmen is a carman. Coffin is a druggist, Mr. Coppers is a plumber, and Mr. Coppersmith is a baker. Mr. Costumer is a cigarmaker. Messrs. Good & Mercy are in the hat trade, but Mr. Hatter

is a shoemaker and none of the Shoemakers makes shoes. Mr.
Monkey deals in monkeys, and other animals, Mr. Oak is a carver,
and Mr. Ode follows the very unpoetical calling of a confectioner.
Mr. Seaman is a tailor, Mr. Tar is a caulker, and Weischman &
Fleischman sell sweet-breads.   Good names for sign-board painters
who work by the foot are those of Calvocoressi and Rodoconachi,
Francis Przygviski and Mr. Reczkiewrez are united in the shoe-
making business.   Mr. Hugueninvuillemin is a watchmaker, Ilium
(George, not "fuit") is a butcher, and Homer is a tailor.   Virtue
is in the book business, Hell a carpenter and Quack a broker.
Byron sells whiskey and Tennyson is an engineer, while Milton is
a news agent and Fielding a druggist.   William C. Bryant is a
Broadway tailor, Happy is a Fifth Avenue tailor, Jolly is a Broadway dyer, John Bull is a moulder, Frenchman makes shoes, Devill
is a painter and Angel a maker of pianos.

To instance a few peculiarities of sign-board literature : Cigars
are described as "segars," "sigars" and "cigarres ;" barber shops
are known as "tonsorial palaces," "hair dressing parlors," "shaving saloons," and "shaving and hair cutting rooms."   The low
concert saloons on the Bowery and Chatham street are all "gardens"
—Belvidere Garden, Olympic Garden, and any number of Volks-
gartens.   One of these places advertises "a high class entertainment by the very best artists in the city."

OUR TENEMENT-HOUSES.

THERE are, according to the records of the Department of Buildings, 21,000 tenement-houses in the city of New York in a
total of 78,000 buildings of all kinds.   Taken all through the city,
the new and the old, the first and the second classes, they average
four stories in height, and are constructed to hold two families and
a half to each floor, or ten families to a house.   Accordingly, if all
these buildings are full, the tenement house population of New
York is 210,000 families, which, at five persons to a family, would
make 1,050,000 men, women and children.   This is evidently an
over-estimate, but certain experienced [agents of tenement-houses
on the east side say that 20 per cent. is all that need be deducted
for houses or parts of houses not occupied.   That deduction leaves
a net tenement-house population of 840,000 souls.

It has been said that the tenements averaged two and a half families to a floor, or ten families to a house, but the population is not at all equally distributed; in some buildings there are as many as five families on a floor, and in others only one or two. Most of the buildings are so built as to effect the greatest possible economy in space, in ventilation and in safety. High and narrow, with contracted hallways and walls of the minimum thickness allowed by the Department of Buildings, with little or no open space in the rear, and frequently a rear tenement building instead of a court, they are hardly bearable as places of habitation in the winter, and still less so in the summer. Indeed, it has become a common sight to see their inmates sleeping, on summer nights, on the roofs of their dwellings or in carts in front of them rather than suffocate within doors. It is their cheapness and their cheapness only that gives them any attraction to the poor, and their cheapness is due to the possibility of packing them with tenants and to the practice of building them on the most economical plan.

The tenement-houses are not, as many suppose, confined exclusively to the lower districts; they are found all over the city and fringe the island on the extreme east and extreme west sides all the way up town. The most fashionable part of New York is flanked by them on either side, and a straight line drawn from Murray Hill to First avenue on the one side and from Murray Hill to Tenth avenue on the other would discover some of the very worst of these dwellings. They are constantly increasing, too; within the past eighteen months 800 new ones have been put up, some down town below Houston street, and others up town as far as Harlem. The distress of the time has not relieved them of their usual class of tenants so much as it has filled them with a new class, which formerly inhabited private houses. The cheaper tenements are better patronized than ever, and land-owners who would not venture to build ordinary dwelling houses to stand vacant are willing to take advantage of the present low price of labor by erecting tenements, which insure a safe and steady, though slow, return for the investment.

The neighborhood of First and Second avenues, between about Twentieth and Thirtieth streets, abounds in tenement-houses of the lower class, inhabited for the most part by Irish and Irish-American working-men, or men who would work if they had the opportunity. The buildings are high and narrow, constructed to hold as many people as possible, without more regard than is compulsory—that is, than is compelled—to health, comfort or safety. In most of these houses there are from fifteen to twenty families, and in some there are more huddled together, and making life bearable as best they can. The crowding would be less tolerable but for the fact that, by their male tenants at least, the tenements are only used almost exclusively for sleeping places. All day the men are away at work, and in the evenings and on Sunday they pass most of their time in the parks or in and around the saloons which flourish in the neighborhood, and of which as one of its features, more will be said anon. In the spring and summer months the women, too, forsake the close buildings for the not much fresher air of the curb-stone and pavements outside. A walk along First avenue, in the locality indicated, after dusk, at this time of the year, will discover the door-steps alive with women nursing their infants and with young girls gossiping among themselves or flirting with the young men; the sidewalk and roadway literally swarming with children screaming and shouting at play, while the scene is lit up by the brilliant lights of the myriad liquor saloons. Evidently the life of this quarter of the city is to be seen principally in the open street, and especially after the close of the working day. The sights and sounds are not at all like those of an American city. They recall rather a Saturday night scene in the back streets of Dublin or in the Irish quarter of London. The names on the shop-windows and sign-boards are, almost without exception, Irish. The conversation of the old people leaves no room for doubt as to their race and origin, and the accent and tone of the younger people tell at once of their descent. There is the good-natured chaffing, the merry laugh and the occasional snatch of a song that are always found in an Irish gathering, and the courtesy to strangers that is characteristic of the Irish people. Many if not most of the people bear unmistakable signs of poverty and the most prosperous looking are prosperous laboring men.

Perhaps the most noticeable feature of this tenement-house district is the extraordinary number of liquor saloons it contains. At a casual glance one would say that there is a grog shop to every five houses; on one block there are no less than seven. These are as different in appearance from the German lager-beer saloons of the lower districts as the people who patronize them are from the German beer drinkers. Instead of the low-roofed, dark basement, with its modest little counter and its sombre proprietor dispensing beer from behind, one seees large, showy stores, brilliantly lighted without and gorgeous within with long mirrors reflecting the array of shining and vari-colored glasses ranged along the counter. The dispenser of drinks is usually a short, thick-set man, with clean shaven face, snowy shirt and high collar, spotless apron and crystal pin, who looks as though he expects to be an "aldhirman from the deestrict." The keepers of these places are, indeed, people of considerable political "influence." Almost without exception they are members ef the district or general commitees of their districts in some one of the various political parties. They are captains of tens and fifties of the retainers of the local political magnates; their "places" are the political headquarters of the various factions in the various election districts, and they are visited periodically by actual or expectant candidates for office who wish to "keep in with the boys." The people who patronize these saloons contrast strongly in appearance with the people who keep them. Visit one of them at almost any time after dusk (Sundays included, though then one must enter by the side door), and the same group will be found. Around the door, and sitting on the boxes and barrels just within, are half a score of idle youths with trousers tight at knee, hat at-one-side, a torn and greasy coat and soiled linen, set oft with the inevitable dollar store pin. At the bar, just entered by the "family entrance," are two or three women, whose dress indicates great poverty, waiting with their tin cans to be served with "a quart of ale, Patsy, for the ould man." On the other side of a stack of empty champagne cases are two or three seedy-looking young men and one maudlin old man drinking 5 cent beer and 10 cent whiskey, and talking politics. The money pours in all the time. Times may be ever so hard, but the saloon does a good business, and the saloon-keeper is an object of respect to his seedy customers, for his word at "the Hall" or with "the Aldhirman" is supposed to be and sometimes is good for a job on "the big pipes" or "at the parks."

IMPLEMENTS OF CRIME.

SINCE the old fashioned modes of robbery by highwaymen and garroters have given place to the scientific burglaries of modern days, a demand has been created for thieves implements, made with all the improvements obtained by means of our advanced mechanical science and increased general facilities. This demand has not been unheeded by that large and influential class of people who are always ready to turn an opportune penny, be it honestly or otherwise, and burglars ot our time and country can boast of having as perfectly finished tools as any reputable workmen. The largest manufactories of burglars' tools are in New York, Philadelphia and the West, and the men who are engaged in the business are frequently of a class who would never contemplate any direct deed of crime. The tools are made partly in one place and partly in another, no maker ever turning out a complete instrument for fear of discovery and consequent trouble. A complete set of tools numbers forty pieces, and is worth from $250 to $400, so that the manufacturers carry on a paying business. It is very difficult to secure the conviction of makers for lack of direct evidence, and even when one is caught the punishment inflicted is not commensurate with the offense. Judge Dowling once convicted a blacksmith and sentenced him to but six months' imprisonment.

One of the best collections of burglar's tools and implements of crime is that which is kept in the Charles Street Police Station. All the articles have been taken from criminals, and most of them have done much service. The collection includes pistols, daggers, knives of every kind, from a common penknife to a huge carving knife, hatchets, axes, swords, canes, slung-shots, brass knuckles, billies, burglars' ladders, jimmies, skeleton keys, masks, fine tooth saws, crowbars and stilettos. Worthy of particular mention is a complete set of brass and steel knuckles found upon Jeremiah Harrington the proprietor of a place on Mulberry street, wherein congregated some years ago a cosmopolitan gang of cut-throats of the worst kind. Harrington himself has been twice tried for murder. A sharp-pointed butcher knife, with a white bone handle, is the instrument with which Donald Magaldo stabbed and killed John Ryland in Baxter Street in July, 1868. A common bone-handled razor, still blood-stained, was used by Amanda Thompson to cut her sleeping husband's throat from ear to ear. Amanda is still spending the rest of her natural life in State Prison. A little two-bladed pocket-knife, which was used by Jack Shannon, the notorious ticket-of-leave man, to cut the throat of John Hastrem in 1866, is also on exhibition here. Shannon fled the country and was never punished for this crime but he is now serving a term of fifteen years' imprisonment.

The collection includes also a large bowie-knife, eighteen inches long, which Richard Somers threw at a little girl on the street; a sword two feet long, part of sword-cane, was the instrument used by Lowenthal in the murder of Hoffman in 1868; a piece of three-ply manilla rope is kept as a memento of three famous executions at which it did service, viz., the hanging of Donnelly in 1868, and of Cline and Wooley in 1869; a large hickory stick, three inches in diameter, covered with fur, was used by two roughs, Murray and Johnson, in assaulting with intent to murder and rob, Mr. Du Bois, while he was carrying $2,500 with which to pay off the teachers in the public schools. Johnson and Murray are both in State Prison. A number of axes have nearly all been used in cases of wife-murder. The axe seems to be, and to have been, from the days of Henry VIII to now, the weapon most popular among husbands who desire to become widowers. All weapons in the Charles Street collection are labeled with the histories attaching to them. It appears from these notes that of one hundred cases of murder there recorded, only about five per cent, of the murderers have been hanged.

Other articles of interest are a black silk mask and beard, worn by a notorious bank burglar, now in jail, and a folding wire ladder used by burglars for scaling from one roof to another, or from window to window. This ladder is so made that it folds easily into a compass sufficiently small to allow of its being carried in a valise or even in an overcoat pocket. There are numerous counterfeit notes and dies found on a counterfeiter who was arrested while at work in Hoboken; a gold badge of peculiar formation with a cutting in strange hieroglyphics, is exhibited as a trophy taken from one of the boldest highway robbers of his day, and a ring of skeleton keys, forty-nine in number, a ring containing almost every description of key used by hotel-thieves, and a kit of burglar's tools found on George Stanley, the infamous English burglar, were all taken from notorious criminals. In a corner by themselves hang a lot of rough-looking instruments used by " Dr." John B. Dennis, a mal-practitioner, in performing an operation upon a woman who died under the treatment.

A portait of Felix Sanchez reminds one that he was arrested in 1859 for killing his father-in-law. He escaped to New Orleans, where, being a negro, he was sold as a slave. Preferring to test the clemency of New York juries to remaining in bondage, he gave himself up for the murder, and was sent to New York for trial. Here he was convicted and sentenced to death, but succeeded in obtaining a stay of proceedings. During this respite he committed a murderous assault upon a keeper, and was sentenced to five years in the State Prison. While serving out this time he became insane, and was sent to the Lunatic Asylum at Auburn, and remained there until recently, when he was transferred to a similar institution on Blackwell's Island.

A COMMUNISTIC BANQUET. *

THE annual Good Friday banquet of the Society of the Refugees of the Commune, held for the purpose of expressing the contempt of that body for the religious observances of the Christian Church, took place at the restaurant of Citizen Clouzot, 136 Bleecker street. The hour appointed for the beginning of the feast was 7.30, and at that time about a dozen French Communists were gathered in the front room, drinking vermouth, absinthe and other liqueurs, smoking cigarettes and discussing the affairs of the day. Prominent among them were Edmond Megy, one of the Communists who, in 1871, assisted at the assassination of Archbishop Darboy and the hostages at Paris ; Olivier, one of the chief writers of *La Cen ralisation*, the Communist organ of this city ; Leblanc, a well-known Communist ; Corny, a Haytian negro Communist ; Mathelot, a veteran French agitationist, and Brossard, the Secretary of the Communist Society. As the writer entered the room Megy glared at him recognizing him as the writer of a recent article in the World on the French Communists in New York, and immediately pointed him out in a very marked manner to his comrades. The writer affected not to notice the attention he had attracted and conversed with a companion; but Megy came up to him and in a threatening manner said: "You fixed me nicely in your article, did you not?"

"And how?"

"Oh, you know," was the reply ; "you were insolent and made fun of me."

"Indeed,"

"Yes, sir, indeed." exclaimed Megy, angrily; "and if I meet you on the street I'll lay you out, and I have a mind to do it now.'

"Well, let us talk about that."

"No, I wont talk about it," was the angry rejoinder, as Megy walked away, his eyes flashing with anger and his friends watching every movement.

A few minutes later word was given to go into dinner, and all present entered the *salle a manger*. The banquet hall was decorated with hangings of very red banners and the flags of the Commune. One bore the inscription, "Vive la Commune;" another

---

* It was for writing this and other articles about the French communists in New York that Megy threatened the author's life, for which offence he was arrested and bound over by Judge F. Sherman Smith to keep the peace. (April 1878).

bore the inscription, "Pas de devoirs, pas de droits," "Pas de droits, pas de devoirs," and "Société des Réfugiés de la Commune." The table was spread with red napkins; most of the guests wore red in some form or the other, and the Chairman, Citizen Mathelot, wore a red shirt. All the guests were in their working-day clothes. Sixteen in all sat down to table, and for nearly two hours were engaged in eating and drinking. The *menu* was about as follows:

Radies.
Potage a la Commune,
Saucisson de Lyon.
Bass a la Blauqui.
Filet de Bœuf aux petits pois.
Rognous sautes au sauce d' 1861.
Pate de Veau a la Rochefort.
Cafe Noir.

Each guest ate heartily and drank as much *vin ordinaire* and cognac as he could hold. The effect of this was noticed as soon as the cloth was removed, when Citizen Mathelot rose and delivered the opening address of the evening. He was greeted with loud applause, and, pulling up the collar of his red shirt and taking from his mouth the clay pipe which he held there, he said: "I do not rise in the character of president for we have no president, and need none. We are all equal. I rise to tell you why we are here; we are here to attest our hatred of the prejudices which make of this a fast day for the poor, while the priests and the rich feast and grow fat. What are these priests? They are the assassins of the people; the enemies of humanity; rascals who always side with the oppressors against the oppressed, with the prosecutor against his victims. (Applause.) The priest has ever been the enemy of liberty—not only the Catholic priest, but the Jewish and Protestant priests as well. In 1851, when the *coup d'etat* came in France, the Archbishop Guibert offered the revolutionists the use of the Church of Notre Dame as a place of refuge from the troops, but, as soon as the *coup d'etat* had succeeded, he opened its doors to sing a Te Deum to Napoleon, and thus allowed his victims to fall into the hands of the assassins. Ah, these priests! I remember when I had a daughter; instead of having her baptized by a priest, I gave her a name and baptized her with wine. A priest afterwards came to me and said he would come and baptize her. I said : 'If you come as a man I will welcome you, but if you come as a priest I will throw you out of the window.' (Loud applause.) Citizens, we do not want these priests. If we get married let us be married by the Mayor. If we must baptize our children let us do it ourselves and in wine, and not let a priest throw his dirty water over its head. (Loud applause.) Those who do not feel and act this way are overinfluenced by their wives or their mothers-in-law. Let them, then free themselves from this influence. Let us feast when these priests fast, fast when they feast—for the Church and its priests are always on the side of property; but sometimes they suffer too, as in the case of M. Darboy." (Loud applause, during which Megy picked his teeth with his fork and smiled triumphantly.)

The next speaker was Citizen Golard, an old man with little hair and much cravat. He said "Citizens, we are here, as Citizen Mathelot has said to express our contempt for the priests. This is right. Take the case of the Archbishop who recently forbade the members of the workingmen's party to enter the church in San Francisco. Ah, if I could have that Bishop by the hair. (Loud applause and wild yells). It is time that we the advance-guard of the people, should come out boldly and express our feelings towards these priests, these assassins of our rights, these robbers of our means. A priests be he Catholic, Protestant or Jew is an enemy and the bishops are the leaders of the people's enemies. (Loud applause).

After this address Citizen Megy was called upon for a toast and said: "Citizens, I propose to you, 'The annihilation of the priests and all other rascals, and the destruction of the Church. Drink!'" This was drunk with due honors amid great enthusiasm, all the guests gazing at Megy with great admiration.

The colored Communist, Citizen Corny, next sang a song, which was loudly applauded, and the Citizen Leblun sang an ode to spring of a lively character, prefacing the third verse with an apology for its religious character, as it contained the line:

J'aime ma mere et mon Dieu——

"Oh, we are indulgent," exclaimed Megy; "go on."

"Yes," exclaimed Citizen Mathelot, "go on; we are not so serious as we look."

Citizen Mathelot then sang a revolutionary ditty, of which the refrain was;

Pon, Pon, Pon,
Courage ! garcons.
P n, Pon, Pon,
Demolissous demolissons.

This excited a degree of enthusiasm, equalled only by that created by a song sung by Megy and entitled "Aux Barricades," of which the refrain was:

Car, il faut-qu'a tout prix nous en soyons vainqueurs.

Citizen Caniare followed with a song of equivocal character which was received with great favor. By this time the claret and cognac, the red flag and the speeches had done their work, and a citizen, whose name was withheld, sang a ditty of such a character that

Mme. Clouzot, who was waiting at the table, left the room in a hurry and the audience saluted its vulgar words and more vulgar refrain with yells of drunken laughter.   At its close the writer left and Citizen Mathelot, leaving his seat at the head of the table, followed him into the hall and asked him to be just in his report. Said the citizen in a tone of maudlin dignity; "Do not repor-what we are, but the principles that we represent;" and as he left the scene, roars of laughter were making the rafters ring at the joke of one of the company, which was much too blasphemous to be printed here.

SATURDAY NIGHT ON THE BOWERY.

A LL the business in New York is not done in stores and offices by any means.   A very large and a very important traffic is carried on out-doors, at the impromptu markets started in all parts of the city to meet the requirements of a class of people whose limited means do not permit them to patronize the regular stores and markets, and who seek the necessities of life in those places where they can buy them most cheaply—to a great extent regardless of their quality.   The locale of the most extensive of these popular open-air marts is on the Bowery, from its beginning to near Grand or Hester Street, and on Vesey Street near Broad-way, and the principal hours of business are from sunset till near midnight on Saturday and holiday nights.   At that time the pave-ment on both sides is skirted with barrows and barrels and various undescribed and indescribable stands of temporary and very un-certain kinds, on which are displayed goods of all descriptions at prices which would make the average householder open his eyes and wonder.   The articles found in the greatest abundance are fruit, vegetables, fish, poultry and miscellaneous household uten-sils.   Chickens tottering on the verge of another world, vegetables which might have been obtained from the Street-Cleaning Depart-ment, fish of week before last, fruit which might have illuminated Sir Isaac Newton about gravitation, all are spread out in threat-ening array under blaring gas or oil lights on ricketty stands the length of the Bowery within the limits mentioned.   The vendors of these commodities are of the roughest and most uncleanly ap-pearance, and their success seems to depend largely upon the strength of their lungs and the amount of their breath.   From sun-down, when they appear, till midnight, when they fold up their shops and quietly wheel away, they keep up a continual halloo. Their patrons, belonging largely to their own ranks, are of ill-clad women, unhappy-looking vagabond children of both sexes, aged respectable and impoverished people who do not get enough to eat, these make up the motley crowd that patronize the out-door market on the Bowery. Their appearance is in strong contrast to the bright exterior of the brilliantly-lighted shops on the street in which the better-to-do people make their purchases, and in which all buy those few articles which the barrow merchants do not keep.

The rivalry between the various stands is hot and close, and the more experienced venders usually do the best business : "Competition, no monopoly," seems to be the favorite sentiment and it is certainly acted up to. Passing quietly along, unheeding and apparently—but only apparently- unheeded, your ears are saluted on one side with a stentorian shout of "New Arabian sugar dates only 5 cents nyarr," and on the other by a whispered and snivelling petition to invest in "Fine fresh lorbsters, all alive nyee." Then a little further on you are free to choose which of a dozen peddlers you will patronize for suspenders, socks, picture frames and a hundred things else, and while you survey the scene and reflect you are jealously watched—watched by a Bowery statue who, with check pantaloons, tight at the knee and wide at the ankle, shoes with three or four steps leading up to the toes, hands in pockets of a short pea-jacket and hat cocked on one side, awaits his opportunity to "go through" you and see "whatcher got about yer."

The occasional bullying of some poor creature who attempts to cheapen the articles which, cheap as they are already, she cannot afford to buy, the squalling of some juvenile thief who has had his head slapped for stealing a handful of nuts, the coarse and ribald talk of the rival venders, are the sounds which, with the jingling of the horse car bells and tramping of the horses' feet, accompany these scenes. Of course they differ widely, according to time and season. This barrow trade fluctuates much more than the regular indoor traffic. It is dependent to a great extent upon the state of the weather, and in times of rain or snow it is considerably reduced. The cosmopolitan features of the traffic, are filled in by three or four Chinamen, who sell what they are pleased to call cigars; a Long Islander with a Turkish cap, which he seems to consider an indispensable adjunct to the horehound candy trade, etc., and, further down towards Chatham Street, by the gentlemen who deal in second-hand clothes, and who, as the night wears on, often get desperate at the lack of custom, lay violent hands upon some passer-by who looks as though he wanted some new clothes, and get their noses, their prominent feature, punched for their trouble.

On Vesey Street substantially the same traffic is carried on and pretty much the same scenes are enacted, only that here, as the street is very narrow, there sometimes occur slight differences between the store-keepers and the barrow merchants in regard to which shall occupy most of the sidewalk, to the great personal discomfort of the passer-by, who does not want the cheese of the storekeeper nor the picture-frames of the peddler. Then a policeman interferes, and after considering which of the two contestants looks most solvent and liberal, decides—impartially. Tea and cheese are the chief articles for sale in the stores on Vesey Street, and crockery and half drunken woman are the principal articles on the sidewalk.

Branches of the barrow trade are established at various points on Eighth Avenue, but they are carried on on a more respectable scale than those on the east side. There the landladies of cheap boarding-houses glide stealthily along, closely veiled, basket in hand, and search for the commodities of boarding-house life at lower prices than they can find in the stores or markets, though they can hardly be compensated by the gain of a few nickels for the constant shocks to their nerves occasioned by the chance apparition of a boarder or of the servant of a rival establishment.

THE CHINESE IN NEW YORK.

There are between 1000 and 2000 Chinese living in New York city. They inhabit chiefly the dilapidated tenement houses in the lowest part of Baxter and Mott Streets. There they have established a sort of Chinese colony, and although in a centre of a dense and mixed population, they manage to live very much by themselves. They have their hotels, their joss-houses or temples, their opium dens, their gambling-houses, and all that goes to make up the pleasures in the life of the average Celestial. The principal opium den is situated in a tenement house at the back of Baxter Street; to reach it one has to cross a dirty and narrow alley known as Donovan's Lane, the scene of several infamous crimes and notably of the manslaughter for which Quembo Ap-po the Chinese desperado, is now serving a term of imprisonment at Sing Sing. On reaching the end of the lane, provided one goes in the evening, the only time to visit China-town, the nostrils are assailed by a strong, sickening odor, which announces that the pipes are bubbling. The scene inside is by no means attractive. In a room measuring about 8x10, opening into another about 5x8, are placed several boards or tables spread with common maitings, and on these lie, all huddled together, Chinamen of all ages and sizes in various stages of dishabille, enjoying the fumes of the drug.

On the occasion of my visit the proprietor of the place, a sickly feeble little man, welcomed me in very good English and bade me sit down. He then threw himself on the table beside the others who were already smoking, and began fixing his pipe. This pipe, made of bamboo, had a stem about two feet long and one inch in diameter. Near the middle of the stem is the bowl, about the size of an egg-cup, in the centre of which is a small hole. The smoker takes a long needle, with which he picks up a little piece of opium out of a thimble or pot, and holds it in the flame of an oil lamp. When it has burned to its proper consistency he smears it over the hole in the pipe, punches a hole through it with his needle and puffs away, sending the smoke first through his lips, then through his nostrils, while all the pipes keep up a bubbling chorus.

The odor of the burning opium is sickening, and this together with the hot air in the close room made me quite faint. But I saw nothing particularly disgusting in the place, nor did I see what so many writers have claimed to describe, "the expression of supreme bliss depicted on the countenances of the smokers." On the contrary, I watched in vain for an expression of any kind on the face of any one of the company. They fixed their pipes and smoked and fell back and fixed their pipes again, with no more expression of "supreme bliss" than a waid politician exhibits when tossing off his whisky. Though I have been several times in the opium dens of the city, I have never seen an opium smoker in a state of insensibility. And I must add, that far from finding the Chinese as dirty as they have been described by the writers on the California press, I have been surprised by their uncommon cleanliness and neatness. Their linen is snowy white, their clothing generally neat, and their apartments, small as they are, always clean and tidy.

But to return to opium-smoking. The pipes used are all imported from China, as well as the little thimbles in which the drug is served out to customers. Opium is worth generally eight dollars a pound, and as the keepers of the smoking-rooms charge 20 and 25 cents a thimbleful, they no doubt make a handsome profit. The opium-smokers who frequent the Baxter Street houses smoke from ¼ an ounce to 1½ ounces a day, for which they pay from 20 to

75 cents. These places are well patronized and are crowded nightly, a room of about, 8x10 frequently accommodating ten or fifteen people at one time.

From the opium-den I went to the joss-house at 34 Mott Street. It is situated in a small, low, but clean room on the third floor. The walls are hung with framed calendars in Chinese characters, and around the room are set three plain wooden benches. At the east end of the apartment is the altar, hung with red satin curtains; attacked to this is a large silk banner, on which are embroidered the figures of the three principal Chinese gods, the gods of Fire Air and Water. Besides these there are scattered around the room, and for use only on special occasions, other gods, and notably Tsoi-Pak-Shing-Kwan, the god of wealth. A temple regulates the number of its gods according to its means, as they are very expensive to get up. On the table are several cedar sticks, which are burned during the ceremonies in honor of the idols, and in front of the altar hangs a perpetual light. All round the room are Chinese lanterns, which are used on festival days only. Careful inquiry revealed the fact that, there being no regular priest in New York, the head man of the gambling-house on Mott Street does duty in that capacity.

At 34 Mott street is the Chinese gambling house, kept in the basement by the man who keeps the hotel upstairs and runs the Joss-house over the road. Fung-Wa is the name of this versatile character. The gambling-house is divided into two rooms, in one of which, at the time of my visit, a wonderful game of dominoes was in progress, while in the other a regular round game was going on. The game of dominees was peculiar. Each man seemed to have about fifty dominoes, and the chief aim of the players seemed to be to make as much noise as possible by slamming them about on the table without any particular object. In the back room about forty men were gathered around a table betting on a game of rather imposing appearance, but being in fact, nothing more nor less than the children's game of "odd or even." The dealer takes a handful of brass buttons and puts them under a sort of sauce-pan-cover, The players make their bets with the banker and among themselves. The dealer lifts the saucepan-cover and picks out the buttons with a long whale-bone, four at a time. When he has picked out the last, the players settle up amid yells and shouting, and the game begins again. On the occasion of my visit the players were betting high and several $50 bills changed hands.

Upstairs is the hotel and restaurant, where Chinese delicacies are dispensed to all comers. The Chinese are great gourmands, notwithstanding their half-starved appearance, and know how to live as well as their neighbors. Among the delicacies of the Chinese cuisine, obtainable here, are cum-chin-gye, or broiled chicken's heart, cum-wah-ham-chi-ho, cr oysters fried in batter with onions, cho-koo-bak-kop-meo-goo, or pigeon stewed with bamboo-sprouts, ki-ton-yu-shee, or sharks fins stewed with ham and eggs. and ha-yuk-kow-chee, or fancy rice cakes made in imita tion of birds and flowers.

The Chinese in New York devote themselves chiefly to the noble professions of cigar-making and clothes-washing, in both of which they are experts. They earn as much money as their neighbors and live on less. They are frugal and industrious, save money smoke opium, gamble, but never get drunk, rarely fight, and take no interest in politics. The police give them a good reputation for peaceableness and good conduct. There is only one Chinese woman in New York, the wife of a cigar-maker; she has several children, all of whom are beginning to speak English. Many Chinamen have found white wives and live happily with them. I had some conversation with a bright, intelligent Irish girl, the wife of a young Chinaman, and she told me that she was well satisfied with her lot. She had been married before to an Irishman, who was killed in a fight, but she preferred her present husband, she said, because he was sober, kind, had plenty of money and did not run after other women; "What more can any dacent woman desire?"

STREET TRICKS.

EVERY large city has its peculiar street scenes and characters. Those of New York are both numerous and interesting. Perhaps no city in the world has more corner fruit and candy stands, peddlers' barrows, organ-grinders, picturesque beggars and professional impostors. There were in 1873 no less than 400 licensed street stands, and as many more not licensed, devoted to the sale of different articles, within the city limits. Since then the number of both classes of stands has more than doubled. This estimate takes no account of the displays made by the keepers of small stores on the Bowery and Third Avenue, who use the sidewalk, rent free, with a charming disregard alike of the rights of citizens and of the corporation ordinances. The owners of street stands are all required to take out a license at the cost of $1, otherwise they are liable to the penalties of the law. Even when they have tui-

filled this requirement they are subject to the whims of the police-
men in their neighborhood, by whom they may at any moment, be
"moved on," and thus have their business broken up.   The
licenses are obtainable only by persons whose applications are en-
dorsed by an Alderman-at-large, or by an Alderman of the district
in which the stands are located.   They are renewable on the 1st of
May of every year, and are granted only with the written consent
of the owners of the premises in front of which the stand is erected
and with the understanding that they shall not project beyond the
stoop line, say four or five feet from the house.   Besides having to
pay for permits, the owners of stands frequently pay the store-
keepers for the privilege of standing in front of their stores.   One
store-keeper on the Bowery has an income of $3,000 ($1,000 more
than his rent) from this source- A man who sells fruit under the
Astor House pays $25 a month for the privilege.   The store-keepers
on Vesey Street also derive large profits from the rental of the sidewalks in front of their stores.   There are nineteen licensed stands
in two blocks on Vesey Street.   It is the duty of the police to arrest
all unlicensed keepers of stands and all licensed keepers whose
stands project beyond the stoop lines, but they do not do it. Flower-
girls are subject to the same regulations as other street merchants
and pay $1, a year for permits, or they are supposed to do so.

The only public venders who do not have to pay licenses are
the newsboys.   The bootblacks are exempt from taxation, and their
polishing profession is open to all comers who have the capital
requisite for the purchase of blacking and brushes, and the physical
strength necessary to keep them from the hands of their Ishmaelit-
ish brethren.

The amount of capital invested in the street candy business
must be very large.   There is hardly a street corner in New York
where chocolate creams and other confectionery are not sold.   In
many respects this line of trade is peculiar to this city.   It certainly is so in regard to the material sold.   In other cities the street-
sold candies are of a much less pretentious order; in other and less
favored places crystallized fruits, preserves and one ounce chocolate
drops cannot be bought at one cent a piece.   There's where we
have the advantage of our neighbors.   In other cities, however, this
line of goods, being sold within doors, lacks the rich incrustation
of dust with which it is usually covered here.   There's where our
neighbors have the advantage of us.   The pea-nut and fruit business generally is very extensive.   It is much pleasanter for the
vender here than it would be elsewhere, in London for example
In that metropolis of an effete monarchy the satraps of the government tyrannically prevent the sale of rotten or unripe fruit.

Here, in this free country, however, we are all at liberty to sell or eat unwholesome fruit to our hearts' content and our stomachs' serious discomfort. It may be in place here to say that it is the opinion of many eminent physicians that a large percentage of our annual summer diseases are the direct results of the consumption of rotten and unripe fruit and vegetables, and of the bestowal of the refuse thereof in the streets and gutters in the poorer quarters of the city, where the rumble of the Street Cleaning Department's cart is seldom or never heard.

Among strange street characters of New York, almost every one must have noticed the large, fat, red-nosed man who sits all the year round on a door-step in Union Square, apparently playing with painted monkeys on sticks and babies' rattles, but in reality offering those articles for sale. The earnest look on the bloated face of this great fellow as he sits all day long with his toy in his hands makes him a very picture of idiocy. The writer has stood looking at that man many times, until he has burst into an uncontrollable fit of laughter. Right by this character, almost any fine afternoon, there may be seen, sitting on the steps of the Wheeler & Wilson sewing machine building, a tolerably good-looking young mulatto woman, dressed in black, and holding in each arm a negro baby in long clothes. What she is there for no one seems to know. No one ever saw her beg or try to sell the babies. Perhaps she is camping out. The organ-grinders of various classes are familiar to New Yorkers. The tall, swarthy Italian, all alone with his instrument of torture, his compatriot with a monkey of doubtful breeding, the married or ostensibly married grinder, who plays upon his organ while his wife plays upon the feelings of passers-by, are all well know to us. Then there are the men and the women who rely chiefly on the meretricious aids to their profession, and carry a small organ and a large family of children of tender years, assorted sizes, on a huge wheelbarrow which carries all their worldly possessions. The ex-military organ-grinder, who hangs his certificate of discharge from the army in front of his organ, used to be a great success, but is now dying out. The old woman with a little one-cent organ, who sits near the theatres at night, is a comparatively newcomer and will not die out at all.

The Bowery and Broadway "statues," with pants tight at knee and wide at ankle, three story boots, hats at one side and arms akimbo, are safest at the greatest distance. We all know them; it is not wise to tackle them with flesh and bone. An equally dangerous character is the tearful and modest young woman whom you find, Niobe-like, dissolved in tears, and who tells you that she is about to be turned out of her room because she cannot pay her

rent and invites you to go with her and judge of the truth of her
story. She belongs to the same class as the young woman who
"Just arrived from Dutchess County," accosts you in a street car,
inquires the way to her "aunt's" and meanwhile finds her way to
your pockets and leaves you a wiser and a poorer man.

WOMEN WHO WORK.

IT has been well said on half the world does not know how the
other half lives, Some cynic has added that it does not care
either: but this is not always true—never true when there are new
phases of toil and suffering to be learned, In the city of New York
alone there are probably a hundred thousand females, ranging in
years from childhood to old age, who depend for their bread upon
the labor of their hands, who, in season and out of season, trudge
to the scene of their work through the snow and slush of winter,
through the heat and dust of summer, in good health, and often in
sickness! The branches of industry in which they are engaged are
manifold. They are employed in textile manufactures and in the
working of metal ; in the preparation of glass, china, ivory, pearl
tortoise-shell, gutta-percha and hair. They assist in the manufacture of willow-ware and carved furniture and upholstery of all
kinds ; they make paper and card-board boxes and bags, and are
very useful in toy factories. They work in printing offices as
press-feeders and type-setters. Their chief employment, though,
is the making of men's and women's wearing apparel, the manufacture of cigars and cigarettes, and the handling of tobacco generally.

In one branch of the manufacture of wearing apparel, the
making of artificial flowers and curling and dressing ornamental
feathers, between 10,000 and 12,000 girls find constant employment.

They are, for the most part, mere children, ranging in ages
from 8 to 14, and their average earning are from $3 to $5 a week.

There are between 1,800 and 2,000 women employed in the
large millinery establishments of the city, and as many more in the
umbrella and hoop-skirt factories. The average weekly earnings
of this class of workers is about $6, and they rarely make more
than $12.

The manufacture of hats- a very important industry, employs
about 20,000 females, and is reasonably remunerative. Hands employed on fur and cloth hats and caps make from $3 to $5 a week
and those working on women's trimmed hats average from $5 to

$15. Some branches of the business are very unhealthy, and the operatives suffer from the inhalation of the dust and coloring matter that is rubbed from the felt.

Nearly 10,000 tailoresses are employed in making "custom work." They are engaged chiefly by the "ready-made clothing" merchants and by the cheap tailors on the Bowery. They are paid from 25 to 75 cents for vests, from 43 cents to $3 for coats, from, 15 cents to $1 25 for trousers, and from $1 to $5 50 for overcoats, and can average from $5 to $11 a week. Much of this kind of work is done at the houses of the workers, and by farmers' wives and daughters, to whom it is peddled out by contractors, and, poorly paid for as it is, it is eagerly sought. A tailor doing a large business on the east side of the city, told the writer, a few days ago, that if he had ten times the work to give out that he has, he could find hands ready and willing to do it all for almost any price, It must be borne in mind that the tailoresses and seamstresses have no Trades' Unions, like the workers of the other and stronger sex, and they have to work for what they can get—or starve. The principal tailoring done by women is on pantaloons, vests, alpaca coats, and linen goods.

Female labor is much used in the cloth factories. One house alone employs 110 girls in this branch of industry. An average of 30 girls are engaged in one room in the weaving of hair-cloth. The labor is hard and unpleasant, and the hair and dust and the odor of stale oil from the machinery make the atmosphere very unhealthy, and tell woefully upon the physical welfare of the hands. The accomodations in these shops are greatly inferior to those in any well-regulated prison work-room. The men and women work together, dress and undress together, and are obliged to eat their miserable midday meals in the foul atmosphere of the shop. For this labor they receive from about $5 to $8 a week, excepting, of course, the old and experienced and rapid workers who make more.

One of the pleasantest occupations for women is that of book-binding. Several thousand women and girls are engaged in it, the majority of the workers being children of between 12 and 15. These are employed only in the lighter branches of the business, such as those of folding and sewing the leaves, laying on the gold leaf etc. At this work they can make from $4 to $7 a week, only the most experienced and rapid hands making more.

One of the most disagreeable female avocations is cigar-making and tobacco manufacturing in all its branches, and yet it employs thousands of respectable young women. They roll and fill cigars, color the bladders for holding snuff, fill, cap, wrap, label, and varnish them. The majority, however, are engaged in " stripping " the tobacco in its leaf form. Naturally the work is very unhealthy, particularly to women of delicate health. Large quantities of the fine dust of the tobacco is inhaled, frequently causing lung diseases and the poisonous vapor exuded by the damp leaf renders the atmosphere of the workshops perfectly stifling. The "strippers," as they are called, average not more than $5 a week, while the cigar-makers, men and women, make from $7 50 to $13 each. Usually the cigars are made by a man and his wife working together, the former doing the rolling and finishing and the latter the stripping and filling.

Thousands of women are employed in the occupation of shirt-making, a very pleasant and fairly profitable work. These average from $6 to $12 a week all the year round. Workers on white shirts make about $8; others on woolen and domestic goods about $6. On fine underwear and fine white shirts their earnings are from $8 to $10 a week, when they are not paid by the dozen. Their average hours of labor are from 7:30 a. m. to 6 p. m., and most of their work is done in the stores. One shirt-house on Leonard street, employs 3,500 hands to conduct its business, and of these at least one-half are women. Seamstresses who go out to work by the day earn from $1.50 to $2 per day and their meals. They are usually good milliners, and competent to do the more difficult sorts of needle-work.

There are several hundred girls and women employed in the large candy factories of the city, where the work is very pleasant and very poorly paid for. The female hands are employed chiefly in packing candies in boxes, wrapping and labeling them, and in putting up bon-bons and other confections. Their pay averages from $4 to $5 a week, the forewomen making as much as $7, and their work lasts twelve hours every day.

POPULAR SONGS.

THE music-publishing business is one of the most interesting and least known of all the trades which find support in this country. It is and always has been in the hands of a very few men who have, in most cases, profited handsomely by the monopoly. I refer particularly to the song-publishing branch of the trade, which is now almost entirely under the control of the Ditsons, W. A. Pond & Co., J. L. Peters, S Br inard's Sons, John Church & Co., and G. D. Russell & Co., and two or three others. The whole number of pieces published in the United States, including both vocal and instrumental compositions, is about eighty thousand. Of this very few, of course, ever attain any considerable sale, indeed, only one song in a thousand ever reaches a sale of one thousand copies, and a composer who averages five hundred copies for each of his songs is considered a success. The song writers of America are very few and they may be classed thus: Hays, of Louisville; Thomas, of New York; Danks, of New York; Henry Tucker, of New York; W. H. Brockway, Harrison Millard, of New York; C. A. White and J. T. Ordway, of Boston, and Root, of Chicago. Having mentioned these, the list is exhausted. Millard and Hays frequently write their own words, but the others usually buy theirs.

It is a remarkable fact that, notwithstanding the large number of amateur poets with whom our land is afflicted, there is but one song-poet in the country worthy of the name. Mr. George Cooper is the man who writes more songs than all others put together, and he needs to write a great many to make the business a paying one, for his remuneration is beggarly, being only from $5 to $10 a piece. This sum appears even more insignificant when compared with the handsome profits made by the music writers. There are, besides him, a number of amateur song-writers who are anxious to furnish words to be set to music, and ask only in return that they may be credited with the authorship, on the title page of the piece. But they find very little occupation, for song-writing requires a peculiar talent, with which few people are gifted. Mr. Cooper possesses this talent in a marked degree, and has written many pieces which have real merit, such as "Dear Little Heart," "When the Tide Comes in," "Learning to Walk," etc.

Of the eighty thousand pieces on the catalogue of the Board of Trade, there are, at present, only about twelve hundred good selling songs and many of these have only just begun to attain popularity. Some of them were sold years ago by their authors at nominal prices and have since become a fruitful source of revenue to the publishers; others leaped into favor with the first edition and have netted their authors handsome profits. Take, for example, Danks' "Silver Threads Among the Gold," which was originally sold for $40 and has since reached a sale of between 300,000 and 400,000 copies and is selling still. "Tramp, Tramp," on the other hand, became popular at once and sold rapidly for over a year, being heard on hand-organs and in brass bands on every street corner, but it has now gone out of fashion and does not sell a dozen copies in a year.

Music-writers like Hays, Danks & Millard, get from $50 to $100

for a s'ng, if sold outright or a commission of ten per cent. on the
total sales, Millard's "Viva l' America" sold over 50,000 copies and
netted about $2,500; his "When the Tide Come in"used to bring
him about $1,000 a year; his "Waiting " averaged 6,000 copies a
year, and his " Under the Daisies " 7,000 copies a year.

Hays' "Mollie Darling " and Hoffman's "Mocking Bird ' have
both had large sales, the first about 500,000 and the second not
quite half as many. The following particulars about the sales of
other popular songs, now made public for the first time, will doubtless prove interesting. J. A. Barry's Little Footsteps, " originally
sold for $5, had a sale of 75,000 copies; "Belle Mahone," 100,000;
J. P. Ordway's "Dreaming of Home, Mother," 50,000; Eastburn's
"How the Gates Came Ajar," 100,000; Hays' "We Parted by the
River side," 100,000; White's "Come, Birdie, Come," 100,000;
Brockway's "Little Sweetheart, Come and Kiss Me," originally
sold for $25 had a sale of 25,000 copies; Warren's "Rock of Ages,"
150,000; Thorne's "Tis But a Little Faded Flower," 75,000; and S.
G. Foster's "Old Folks at Home," 400,000.

Of Covert's famous song, "The Sword of Bunker Hill," 100,-
000 copies have been sold; of Wallace's "Sweet Spirit Hear My
Prayer," nearly 500,000 copies, and of Work's famous temperance
song "Father, Come Home," 250,000

Of the popular American comic songs, Howard's "Shoo Fly"
sold 200,000 copies; C. A. White's "Put Me in My Little Bed,"
which I do not hesitate to class as comic, 100,000; Harrigan & Hart's
Mulligan Guards," originally sold by the authors for $50, 100,000;
Harrigan & Hart's idiotic "Hildebrandt Montrose," originally sold
for $25, 200,000 copies. The popular English comic song, "Pull
Down The Blinds," sold 50,000 copies in this country within a few
months.

England, which is *par excellence* the home of comic music
has sent us many popular songs, or rather we have taken them.
As there is no international copyright law, the music publishers
are at liberty to sell them without giving the authors or the original publishers any compensation. Among the English songs thus
naturalized are: Sullivan's "Let Me Dream Again," which sold
100,000 copies; "Champagne Charlie," 75,000; "Good-bye Charlie,"
50,000; "What are The Wild Waves Saying?" "Won't You Tell Me
Why, Robin ?" 100,000; and "Five O'Clock in the Morning,"
250,000.

POLICE DETECTIVES.

THE stranger in New York little thinks, as he enters his hotel or saunters into a theatre, that his every movement is noted by a lynx-eyed detective, who, dressed in ordinary clothes, and these usually of the best kind, lounges at the entrance. He little imagines that the benevolent-looking old man, who leans on the hotel counter talking to the clerk, is one of the most trusted officers of the secret force, and is perhaps wondering to himself if he has ever seen the stranger's face before, and, if so, where? Still less does he suppose that the handsomely-dressed young man, standing chatting with the manager at the theatre door, is detailed there by the police to watch for pickpockets and the like. Yet such is the fact. The detectives are everywhere and no one seems to know them, except the thieves, the officers who have dealings with them, and the newspaper men, who know everybody. Stand with me some evening at the entrance to Booth's Theatre, as the people are going in, and keep your eyes and ears open. A respectable-looking old gentleman, quietly dressed, and with a ticket for a reserved seat in his hand, walks along, and, as he reaches the gate, a handsome young man at my side taps him on the back and says familiarly, "Ah Jim, where are you going?"

Jim starts, as well he may; for he is one of the most notorious pickpockets in the country, and replies uneasily: "Oh, I am just going to see the play; all right I suppose."

"Oh, I guess you don't want to go to-night," suggests the young man, and the respectable-looking old gentleman turns sadly away.

A minute later, the attention of the young man at my side who, it is needless to say, is a detective, is attracted to a studious looking youth with spectacles, whom he salutes with "Hollo, Tom, where have you been?"

Tom turns and stares, looks surprised, as indeed he is; for he has been absent from New York for five years, and did not expect to be recognized. "Hush," he say; "Yes 'its me. What's up?"

"Where are you going?" asks the detective.

"Want to see the show, that's all," is the reply; "no business, you can let me in."

"Honest injum?" asks the detective; "Yes, honest injum," is the answer.

"Well, go ahead," says the officer; "but mind, I will hold you responsible for any thing that is done in your line."

"O. K.," says the studious youth and passes on with light and careless step.

The Police Detective force of New York is a comparatively new institution. Up till as late as 1844 the only police in the city were the night watchmen, who were known as "Old Leather-heads," because they wore large leather hats like those of the fire-men. In those times what detective service there was to be done was intrusted to the city marshals or sheriffs appointed by the mayor, of whom the most famous were Jacob Hayes, A. M. Smith, and John Burleigh. Hayes has always been regarded as the original New York detective.

In 1844, under the administration of Mayor Harper, the Municipal Police, or as they were commonly called the M. P's were organized. Mr. Matsell became their chief, and in 1845 he detailed three of them to "special duty" at head-quarters. Other assistants he had who were called "aids to the chief," but these three Mr. Matsell dubbed "shadows." They were in fact detec-tives, and were principally engaged in hunting up bank-thieves, who then formed a very-large part of our criminal classes. In 1846-7 the "shadows" were reinforced by the addition of three more, one of whom was Walling, the present superintendent.

But it was not until 1857, when the Metropolitan Police were established, that New York had a regular detective force. A de-tective bureau was then founded as a part of the new institution, having an office at Police Head-quarters. In 1858, Mr. Walling was made chief of detectives, and the bureau was organized pretty much as it now is. The force now consists of eleven regularly de-tailed men, and about as many more on probation, that is to say, assigned temporarily, until they show what they are worth. The men are selected from the ranks of the police because of their special aptitude for detective work. Besides these, there are the "ward detectives" who do duty in their respective precincts and are appointed by the police board on the recommendation of the captains.

The pay of detectives, which is the same as that of patrolmen, viz: $100 a month, seems inadequate to the work they are expected to perform, which is frequently of a very delicate nature, requiring much tact and intelligence, and sometimes involving considerable expenditure of money. As the police board has no power to pay their expenses, they have to do so themselves, unless the parties interested in the case are willing to assume them. As a rule, people interested in the arrest of criminals defray the expenses of detectives who have to leave the city; otherwise very few criminals would ever be captured by New York officers outside of New York.

The police detectives undertake no businessexcept of a criminal character and attend to no crimes except those committed in New York city. If they were to attend to all the complaints of jealous wives and husbands, to all the romances of ill-used children and unnatural parents, or if they were to respond to all the calls for their services outside of the city, they would have ten times more than they could do. But they leave all these matters to the private detective, who, as he undertakes no work without a liberal retainer in advance, can afford to give his time to matters of purely personal or foreign concern. Some of the cases which come into the hands of the regular New York detectives occupy years of labor to complete, some of them never are completed. The small force at present employed in the department is barely able to cope with nearly 20,000 professional criminals resident in this city. The detectives know many of them, but, unfortunately, they know the detectives too. The present management of the detective bureau, however, has considerably lightened the work of the officers and largely reduced the danger to be feared from the criminal classes,

When a malefactor is arrested, he is first taken to police headquarters and conducted to the detective room, where he is examined for identification. He is weighed, examined and searched, and all possible inquiries are made in regard to his antecedents. The chief then notes down, in what he calls his "Pedigree Book," the name and aliases of the prisoner, his height, weight, color of hair, color of eyes, peculiarities of features, and any distinctive marks on his body. He adds all that is known of his habits, previous arrests, and other matters of interest, so that he is rapidly compiling a biographical and descriptive dictionary of all the thieves in the country. This done, the prisoner is sent to have his photograph taken. Often he objects to this operation, and, by closing his eyes, distorting his features and making himself as obstreperous as he can, seeks to prevent it. But the police are used to these tricks, and usually succeed in tiring their man out, and securing the picture at last.

These useful works of art are then added to the rack constituting the so-called Rogues Gallery, which is composed of 1,500 photographs of criminals of various degrees of turpitude, placed in a rack in the detective bureau. They are all numbered to correspond with the number on the biography in the Pedigree Book. They are also kept in duplicate to be sent to detectives in other cities if the originals should chance to emigrate, and recently the office has adopted a plan of exchange, by means of which it sends copies of its pictures to detectives and chiefs of police all over the country, and receives others from them in return. By this means, if the plan is properly carried out, it will soon be difficult for a thief to go anywhere in our large cities without being recognized and "spotted."

Another precaution of the detective office is to make a thief, who practices in any special line, known to his particular victims. I was in the office a few days ago with the chief of the bureau, when Bill Connolly—a notorious hotel-thief, who had just been arrested at the Astor House in the very act of leaving the room which he had been robbing—was brought in and identified. Before he was taken to court to be committed, the sergeant sent for the most prominent hotel-keepers in town, and showed his prisoner, so that, in case they might ever encounter him, they would be on their guard. Hardly had Connolly been taken away, when two detectives arrived with another hotel-thief, who had just been arrested at the Fifth Avenue Hotel, and sent up by the district attorney for investigation. He had never been caught here before, or at least no one recognized him; but his countenance and demeanor should have been enough to convict him. He struggled and fought to prevent himself from being measured and weighed, and was finally handcuffed, and removed by force to the photographic gallery.

The hotel thief is one of the most dangerous of thieves. To the detectives he is known as a "hotel dancer." His mode of operation is very simple. He goes to a first-class hotel, takes a room and proceeds at once to study the habits of the guests, paying particular attention to those who go to bed under the influence of liquor. These he marks for his own, and, with his feet encased in carpet or list slippers, he pays them nocturnal visits for professional purposes. Often he calls for a newspaper in the morning, and, walking up and down the corridor, apparently engrossed in the news of the day, watches his opportunity, and, when one of the guests leaves his room for an instant, darts in and captures his booty. Most of these light-fingered gentry are of respectable appearance, and it takes an experienced eye to detect their tricks.

Some thieves have their own peculiar styles of work, which no one else can imitate. A few years ago, there was a female pickpocket who used to "work" the Broadway line of cars. Her mode of operation was to sit down by some wealthy-looking old gentleman, drop her handkerchief, allow him to pick it up, engage him in a quiet flirtation, and, while his attention was distracted pick his pocket. She was a beautiful woman, and for a long time she puzzled the detectives, but at last she was caught and only escaped because the victim would not prosecute. After that, however, whenever a theft was committed on the cars in her peculiar way, her movements were watched. It was thus that she finally obtained her deserts, and she is now serving a term in the state's prison-

In the case of burglaries, the detective's task is rendered comparatively easy if he can only find the tools used in the job, because there are very few manufacturers of burglars' implements, and they are nearly all known to the police. Having once learned the maker of the tools used, the detective goes to work to discover who has bought such or such an article, and, having ascertained this, he knows just whom to look for. In this connection it may be said that burglars' tools are altogether peculiar and are made specially for purposes of crime, but, as I explained in a recent article on this subject, it is difficult to punish the makers, owing to the precautions they use to conceal their employment.

A large part of the detective's time is employed in hunting up and recovering stolen property, and this used to be a difficult and tiresome task. It has been much simplified, however, of late, by the adoption of what is known as the "Postal-Card System." As soon as a robbery is reported at head.quarters, a description of the stolen goods is printed on postal-cards and sent round to pawn-brokers and others.

It is impossible to tell a thief by his or her appearance, and in this respect the detectives, knowing their game intimately, have an advantage over the public generally. One afternoon, last winter, a Fifth Avenue stage, standing at the Fulton Ferry, with ten passengers inside, was just about to start, when Detective Dorsey, one of the brightest of officers, in citizen's clothes, poked his head in at the door and said: "Look out, ladies and gentlemen, there are two pickpockets inside!"

Naturally, the passengers looked very uneasy and fidgeted around. After an awkward pause, an old gentleman, wearing the dress of a minister and carrying a book under his arm, got up, and saying, "Dear, dear, I don't want to ride with pickpockets," got out. He was followed by an old gray-haired lady, dressed in deep mourning, who, muttering, "Nor I, either," stepped down, too.

As this respectable couple disappeared, the detective put his head in again, slammed the door, and shouted, "All right, they have left," and the stage rumbled away.

FANNY STACY'S MOTHER.

WHEN the steamship City of Chester arrived at this city from
Liverpool a few days ago, it had on board, among the cab-
in passengers, a good-looking woman of about thirty-five or forty
years, and an old lady who looked fully eighty, and who bore on
her face undoubted signs of trouble or of dissipation most unusual
in women of her apparent position in life. Attaching to these two
women is a somewhat remarkable story.

Many years ago there lived in a large town in Virginia a man
of considerable means and of good social and business repute —
Stacy by name and an ironmaster by trade. He had married early
in life a handsome girl of Irish descent, by whom he had four children. It was currently reported that the man did not live happily
with his wife, and after the birth of their fourth child Mr. Stacy,
unable longer to bear with the habitual and incorrigible intem-
perance of his wife, instituted suit for divorce and, meanwhile,
separated from her, taking the children into his own care. Pending the suit for divorce Mrs. Stacy went to England to stay with
relatives residing there, and shortly after, Mr. Stacy, reading in
one of the English papers, of her death, stopped the proceedings
for divorce, and, a few months after, married a young lady living
in Richmond. Mr. Stacy had three children by his second wife,
with whom he led a happy and contented life, and he was much
grieved when, after a lapse of ten years, she died in childbirth,
leaving him for the second time a widower. This grief, however,
was apparently not inconsolable, for after a short period of mourning he moved to New York and married a third time. By this last
marriage he had four children, three boys and a girl. After a
short residence here Mr. Stacy returned to Virginia.

In 1873 Fanny Stacy, the eldest child by the first marriage, and
by all reports a very estimable young person, went to England on
a visit for the benefit of her health. While staying at Torquay
she met an old lady who had known her father and mother in
America in the early days of their married life, and from this person she learned, to her surprise and dismay, that her mother, Mrs.
Stacy No. 1, was not dead, but was living in London in very poor
circumstances, to which she had been reduced by her habit of ex-
cessive drinking. Miss Stacy took no particular steps to verify this
report, but on her return to America told her father what she had
heard. The old gentleman was incredulous and particularly angry

that any one should have dared to mention the name of his disgraced wife to her daughter. He refused to take any measures to find out the truth, and from that time displayed great coldness towards Fanny, who, at this time, was the only surviving child of the first marriage.

In the early part of 1875 Mr. Stacy, who had been in bad health a long time, died. When his will was opened it was discovered that by a codicil, added the year before, he had revoked all bequests to Fanny Stacy, and left the whole of his fortune, amounting to over $1,000,000, to the children by the second and third marriages and to his surviving widow.

By advice of a lawyer, a friend of the family, Fanny determined to contest the will. To do this successfully, it was necessary to find the first wife of Mr. Stacy, prove the first marriage, the consequent illegality of the other two marriages and the illegitimacy of all their issue. Miss Stacy, therefore, started in April last, in company with an old friend to England in search of her mother. For months she searched and advertised and sought in vain; no sign of her mother was to be found nor any news of her to be learned. A few months ago, though, she engaged the services of some experienced English detectives, and by their aid succeeded. She found her mother in a hut in the very lowest part of London, inhabited by the poorest classes of Irish laborers, living a disgraceful life of continual intoxication. The mother recognized her daughter by her striking resemblance to her father, and after much persuasion and earnest entreaty, consented to go to America and reform her life, help her daughter to get what was due her and to get her own share. The old lady was taken from her squalid abode, well and decently clad, taken to Liverpool and put aboard the City of Chester, bound for New York. On the voyage she was seriously ill owing to her sudden and total deprivation of all intoxicating drinks, which Fanny Stacy had absolutely and firmly refused to allow her. However, she rallied and got through all right, landed safely in New York, and started with her plucky daughter for Virginia, where the suit is now pending to set aside the will of the late Mr. Stacy, ironmaster, of Virginia.

BOARDING-HOUSE LIFE.

OF about eighty-two thousand buildings in the city of New York nearly twelve thousand, without counting 127 used as hotels, are occupied as boarding houses. Of these a large number are regularly licensed sailors' and immigrants' houses ; but the most of them are used for general purposes, and may be classified as first-class or fashionable boarding-houses; second-class boarding-houses, for persons of moderate means and immoderate pretensions, and third-class, or mechanics' and poor clerks' boarding-houses. These three classes of dwellings are kept by all sorts of people, who, provided they do not wish to avail themselves of the hotel law, are not required to take out licenses and are at liberty to carry on business when and how they chose. They have increased largely in number during the past few years, partly owing to the high rents exacted in this city, which render it practically impossible for persons with modest incomes to keep house, and partly out of the growing indisposition of people to assume the cares and responsibilities of housekeeping when they can avoid them so cheaply and so reasonably as they now can.

The fashionable boarding-houses are confined to no particular neighborhood; they abound on the side streets in the neighborhood of Fifth avenue and even encroach upon that fashionable thoroughfare, principally below Thirty-fourth street. They are to all appearance private dwellings; it is only by going inside that one gets at their real character.

Take, as a specimen, one kept by a widow lady assisted by her married daughter and three single daughters. Mrs. W., the old lady, is the relict of a distinguished lawyer who died comparatively poor, and she, having quarreled with his family, and her eldest daughter, Mrs. M., having made a mesalliance, were obliged to take boarders. The girls are all good looking, well educated and accustomed to good society, so, upon the death of the father, it was decided to take a large house up town and receive a few gentleman boarders—but gentlemen only. Operations were begun, and before long five young men, all of good position, were comfortably installed, paying an average of $12 per week for board and lodging. Mrs. W. was soon a favorite with all, and Mrs. M. might have been, but for several reasons was not. First of all she worshipped Dick. Dick was her husband, a worthless vagabond, who was always away and always wanting money. Him she adored and him she held up as a model to all the boarders, and sang his praises at breakfast, dinner and tea. Then she was always sending Dick money, and was consequently in a state of chronic impecuniosity herself, and to remedy this she was wont to borrow money of her boarders, or at least of one of them, a good-natured, easy-going fellow, who could not refuse (who could?) to advance a few dollars to the sister of three charming girls who had evidently seen better times. And as Mrs. M. was hard up, and the dinner proportionately poor, the ladies would endeavor to compensate for the poverty of the menu by dilating; upon their former greatness and the past glories of their late Uncle Ben. Then the young ladies, who in the days of their former prosperity had attended the Charity Ball, were never tired of telling of the dresses they used to wear, and the gentlemen they used to dance with. Mrs. M. was always most aristocratic when she had borrowed some money, and the girls were always most patronizing when they had bet gloves on something they could not possibly lose on, and Uncle Ben and his numerous excellent qualities were recited abundantly. When Mr. Brothers came home from a wedding and spoke of the beautiful floral decorations he had beheld, the sisters heard him out, [and [in chorus went him several better in their description of the floral tributes which decorated the coffin of their defunct Uncle Ben. When the dinner was poorest Mrs. M. would enliven the drooping spirits of her boarders by reciting the good things which decked the breakfast-table on the occasion of her wedding. And so on, to the chapter's end. A more patient, a longer-suffering set of gentlemen than the boarders at Mrs. W's and Mrs. M's are rarely met with. They put up with poor meals, worse attendance and the worst imposition for months, and all because they felt a genuine sympathy for gentlewomen in distress. But at last the climax came. Dick came home and bullied his wife and quarreled with the boarders, who were totally neglected for his sake. He quarreled with his sisters-in-law, and made himself so generally obnoxious that one by one the boarders left and sought other quarters, all inwardly vowing that they would never again take board with a family which had "seen better days."

Of course there are others of the first-class boarding-houses where few or none of the trials at Mrs. W's are met with, but these are mostly of the strictly humdrum, respectable kind, carried on in the style of private or family hotels. The inmates are frequently well-to-do married people, occupying a suite of rooms to each family, eating at separate tables, and leaving each other as severely alone as possible. The life in houses of this sort is, as far as can be seen by the casual sojourner, as dull and uneventful as in an apartment or French-flat house. There being no common sitting-room nor dining-table there is very little opportunity for the happening of those incidents, and interchange of those amenities which render regular boarding-house life invariably diverting to say the least of it.

The second-class boarding-houses abound on the far west and far east of the side thoroughfares between Fourth and Fiftieth streets. Their rates, varying not so much according to accommodations as in proportion to the anxiety of the applicant to live in any given district and in proportion to the self-confidence in the landlady, run all the way from $5 to $10 per week for single rooms and board, with "fires invariably extra." These places are usually kept by widows, or, if the keeper has a husband, he is usually of the same stamp as Dicken's Mr. Tibbs and does not count. The widows have almost invariably, according to their own accounts, "seen better days" and been "suddenly reduced in circumstances," or they are "not regular boarding-house keepers," but having houses too large for their small families "receive a few select guests for a moderate compensation." The landlady wishes to be looked up to and respected as a hostess, not patronized and tolerated as a housekeeper—and she usually has her way.

Enter the house of Mrs. Brymmens on Forty-fourth street. The boarders are at dinner. Mrs. Brymmens presides. She is a tall, bony, angular woman of about forty, not bad-looking, but too strictly proper in appearance to suit an ordinary person. Rumor says she had a husband once, and no one can say she had not. But nobody ever saw him, living or dead. Mrs. Brymmens rarely speaks of him, but certain mysterious hints she drops at times have led to the acceptance of a sort of tradition in the house that he was an officer in the Federal army during the war and was killed in battle. Mrs. Brymmens strengthens this idea by occasionally waxing unduly patriotic in the cause of the Union and unnecessarily severe in denunciation of traitors. Next to Mrs. B. is the doctor, as he is called. The doctor is a clerk in a wholesale drug-store, hence his title and hence his assumption of medical gravity and professional dignity when a fellow-boarder sprains his ankle or cuts his finger. The doctor's neighbor is a Mrs. Wynne, wife of a commercial traveller, who is away ten months in the year. Mrs. Wynne is very amiable and slightly aristocratic when Wynne is away, and slightly amiable and very aristocratic when Wynne is at home. She knows every distinguished man, woman and child in the town, and has a way of speaking of all entertainments she attends as having "been patronized by the eclat of the town, and gone off with great elite" (pro-

nounced elight). Mr. Sonet, a merchant, and Mrs. Sonet, who
always call each other "dearest" at the table, and are heard quar-
reling loud and often in their own room; Miss Sonet, who plays
with the piano, and sings a' the boarders, and is always expect-
ing an offer and never gets it, and three young men of the usual
boarding-house stamp fill up the other places. Wynne happens
to be home to-day and in very bad humor. He frowns at the
soup; Mrs. Brymmens asks about the condition of the South. He
smells suspiciously at the fish; Mrs. Brymmens suggests that the
Centennial will be a glorious affair. Wynne does not answer, but
turns his attention to the doctor and asks if the weather is not
very unhealthy? The doctor makes a long address on that fruitful subject, and Sonet tries to put in a word, but every time he
opens his mouth Mrs. Sonet asks him to pass something, and
thus succeeds in keeping him quiet. The dinner progresses,
when Mrs. Brymmens is called from the room. Miss Sonet is
asked to take the head of the table; she does so, and Mr. Brown,
a young man with a grandfather who won't die, takes occasion to
pay her a compliment on the grace with which she presides. The
doctor snubs him, but Miss S. looks pleased, grins, and tries to
blush, and goes upstairs after dinner, convinced that Brown is
"going to speak."

And so on from day to day. If a boarder is punctual in paying his bills, he may grumble; if unpunctual, he may not. If a
man has a wife and pays board for two, he ranks above a single
man, and may grumble and bully twice as much; if he has a wife
and daughter, and pays board for three, he may bully and grumble three times as much. On Sunday everybody wears his or her
best; turkey (with hot cranberry sauce, a characteristic boarding-
house abomination), takes the place of the week-day joint, and
Mrs. Brymmens substitutes religious sentiment for patriotic fer-
vor, and asks diligently about the sermons, while Mrs. Wynne
asks patronizingly who was on the Avenue, and if there were any
handsome dresses.

When a new boarder comes into the house, be it a gentleman
or lady, that person is regarded with great suspicion, and for a
few days, at any rate, all the old boarders keep close together, get
uncommonly intimate, and conspire, by rude staring and stage
whispering, to make the new comer as uncomfortable as possible.
The landlady introduces her new guest to all the others on the
first opportunity, taking occasion to accompany each introduction
with a brief biography of the person introduced. This she often
supplements afterwards with mysterious hints as to the family
connections and business prospects of her guests, which leaves

the stranger in a more uncomfortable condition than ever, until
by companionship and that close intimacy which is the most objectionable feature of boarding-house life, he gets to know everybody's business and everybody gets to know his, and mutual regard or mutual contempt is engendered, when everything goes on
as usual.

Apart from the characters here lightly portrayed, there are
the servant girl and colored waiter who, whether by reason of having so many masters and mistresses, or because of the familiar relations which usually obtain between them and the boarders, are
more impertinent, lazy and general worthless than even in any
hotel. They read your letters, feel the weight of your trunk,
count your linen, examine inscriptions on the backs of your pictures, steal your cologne, purloin your powder, borrow your books,
insist upon regarding all the loose change in your pockets as their
rightful perquisites, Life in boarding-houses would not be quite
half what it is if boarding-house servants could be abolished by
act of the Legislature.

The third-class boarding-houses, the houses of poor clerks and
other impecunious persons, are found chiefly in the neighborhood
of Bleecker and Macdougal streets, near Washington square, and
in the side streets below Fourteenth, all the way between Second
and Ninth avenues. Their rates for board and single room average $6 per week, and are usually payable in advance. Houses of
this class are kept by widows of limited means, men with small
business and smaller capitals, broken-down hotel-keepers and
others. They are vulgarly known as "hash-houses" owing to the
great popularity, at least among the proprietors, of the dish expres-
sively called "hash." In the higher circles of life this dish is often
euphemistically called "ragout;" but among the simple folks now
under consideration it is plain "hash"—and they have plenty of
it. Not to put too fine a point upon it, their whole existence may
be discribed as a sort of hash in which the good, bad and indif-
ferent are so indiscriminately blended as to produce a tolerably
passable, and altogether unique whole. The better side of human
nature is seen oftener in these unpretending boarding-houses than
in those of the higher classes. And if some of the boarders do sit
at table in summer without their coats, and if the lady boarders
do come down to breakfast sometimes with their hair in curl-pa-
pers, and if the boarders do put their knives in the butter and into
their mouths, and do put their elbows on the table, there is, nevertheless, a great deal of good to be found in these places. Many a
poor clerk out of employment has had cause to be thankful to his
andlady for the long credit she has given him, and the free

board and lodging he has got from her when he was unable to pay for it. And these landladies have a great deal to bear from the class of people they deal with. It is considered legitimate sport among a certain class of blackguards to cheat boarding-house keepers, and many a poor woman, struggling hard for a living, has been the victim of what are known to the profession as "boarding-house bilks." For, unless a boarding-house is regularly licensed under what is known as the hotel law, the keeper cannot legally detain a boarder's luggage and effects for an unpaid bill, and even if he could it would generally be found that by the time the landlady's patience was exhausted, or perhaps long before, all the convertible effects of the delinquent boarder had been stealthily removed and converted into cash, either at a pawnbroker's or at a second-hand clothing store. To sue would, of course, be useless, and so the boarding-house keeper is not unfrequently the victim of well-meaning but impecunious persons and of regular swindlers, who, to use their own phrase, "find moving cheaper than paying rent."

SOME CURIOSITIES OF CRIME.

THE question of crime is always an interesting study, and its causes and peculiarities, in a city like New York, where it is constantly and steadily on the increase, cannot fail to prove instructive and profitable reading to the student of social evils, and their possible remedies.

From the published criminal statistics it can be seen that, while it is impossible to tell the exact number of persons that might be classed as habitual criminals in our city population, it is indisputable that, counting up the number of prisoners of the rank of felons in our State prisons, the class is found to be increasing immensely, and the percentage of criminals to the population increases much more rapidly than the normal increase of population by immigration and birth.

The increase of crime is attributed to the increasing density of the population in the city and the influx of persons who live by crime, and who immigrate every year. This being the richest State in the Union, and having the greatest facilities for crimes against property, the criminals from other states and other countries make it their residence to a great degree, and their temporary sojourn in a greater measure. The records of the Prison Association show that the proportion of foreign-born criminals is not only in excess, but the crimes against property are connected with that class of prisoners who seem to have floated into this State as criminals, that is, cracksmen and burglars. Then come in the boys, the youth who are born among us mostly, that is, from among us more than from the rural districts. When they are traced back to their homes, they are found not to have sprung up from the well-educated and the well-housed; but the region south of Fourteenth street, for example, and the tenement-house districts, the district-dens of the city, have actually been the birth places of a very large proportion of these criminals that we now find in the penitentiaries and State prisons. The younger criminals seem to have come almost exclusively from the worst tenement-house districts, that is, when traced back to their homes in this city. The Sixth Ward, Little Water Street, Cow Bay and the Five Points, have graduated some of the very worst criminals ever known to the law, and, though these localities have been somewhat improved of late years, they are still pest-holes of crime and immorality. Wherever improvements have been made, they have been followed by a proportionate decrease in crime.

On this question of the connection of crime and tenement houses the Superintendent of the House of Refuge gives some interesting facts. Of 500 houses, residences of criminals, recently visited, 410 were tenement houses. These places were occupied by many families, having numerous children, and the rooms were usually unclean, and in some cases filthy. From ten to twenty families are frequently found under one roof. One house was found, occupied by thirty-two families, having in the aggregate ninety-six children. The influence of these houses and their surroundings upon their inmates can well be imagined. It shows itself, not only in the prevalence of gross immorality and the frequency of predatory crimes, but it adds to the already sickening details, published from time to time, of the heredity of criminal character. The ignorance, brutality, habitual crime, and utter infamy which continually make the dark places of the city dangerous and forbidding, and which are visible plague spots in our city life, mark the very name and record of social and physical causes of degeneration and prominent vices, with which society never interferes sufficiently nor soon enough. For it is not mere punishment of the criminal that we want. To remove the stigma of perpetual and professional wrong-doing on the part of a large proportion of our population, we must remove the causes.

It is positively alarming to note the immense proportion of

refuge boys among the criminal classes, refuge boys who have been
sent to so-called reformatory institutions to be made honest, and
usually emerge from them ten times worse than ever.   Dividing
the total number of criminals into two classes, those who are not
refuge boys and those who are, we find that 63.83 per cent. of the
former are habitual criminals, while the latter show 93.15 per cent.
It thus appears that, while refuge boys constitute a little less than
one-fourth of the prison population for all crimes, they furnish
29.41 per cent. of the habitual criminals, or nearly one-third. Com-
paring crimes against property with the total number of crimes of
refuge boys, we find that 79.45 per cent. of the latter class of prisoners, and that 90.56 per cent. of the refuge boys, in prison, are
under sentence for crimes against property.   The figures in a like
comparison for crimes against the person are 20.55 per cent. of the
latter to 9.44 per cent. of the refuge boys, or less than one-half.
As to the career and ancestral characteristics of these boys, we
find that the average at which their childhood was neglected is
8 1-4 years, they began crime at 9 years and 8 months, and they
went to the refuge at 12 years and 9 months. Moral degradation
began at an average age of 14 years and 9 months, being 1 year and
6 months earlier than the average of other criminals. They contracted disease at 19 years and 6 months. Dr. Harris reports a
case of a boy who began a vicious life at 6 years of age. At 5 he
was a neglected child, running wild in the streets of New York,
the victim of the licentiousness of an abandoned woman at 6, in
the House of Refuge at 9, in the Poor House at 10, with his mother
and sisters, and beginning the career of a drunkard at the same
age, his parents being both habitual drunkards as well as himself.
Both his parents are habitual criminals, his father having served
two terms in State prison and two in the Penitentiary. This boy
has since become demented. What romance could possibly sur-
pass in horrible fiction the ghastly reality of this brief career?

The officers of the Prison Association recently made, and are
still making a manly fight against what they very properly consider one of the chief causes of the increase of crime, viz.: the in-
discriminate herding together of prisoners of various ages and of
various degrees of moral turpitude in such close proximity that
the mere beginner in crime is soon totally corrupted by the old
stagers. Though this practice is against the law of the State, it is
common in all our city prisons. In the Tombs two and even three
men are crowded together, into a cell barely large enough for one.
In the Raymond Street Jail in Brooklyn the practice is even worse,
for here old men and little boys are left together, unwatched, in a
dark corridor outside their cells, and on the other side, old women

and little girls, and women with babies at their breasts are mixed
up in one conglomerate mass of filth, dirt, crime and obscenity,
and God help the beginner in crime who is forced once to inhale
this damnably noxious atmosphere.   There are instances without
number of the criminally cruel effects of this imbecile course, instances of boys arrested for throwing stones or for some other
trifling offense, thrown into jail with some old thieves, from whom
they have learned the first step to the State prison; instances of
little girls, innocent of serious offences, suddenly thrown into
close intimacy with abandoned women and emerging with them
into a life of shame.   Can any crime for which a prisoner can be
punished equal in downright wickedness the great and unpardon-
able crime of the authorities who permit such things as these to
pass under their eyes?

OUR BOHEMIAN COLONY.

THERE are settled in New York between 15,000 and 18,000 Bohemians, people whose modes of life, opinions and political
sentiments differ so widely from those which obtain among some
other foreign residents as to deserve special notice.   They are
more clannish than other foreigners and more tenacious of their
national manners, customs and language than even the Germans
of the working classes.   The New York Bohemians live entirely
among themselves, and the neighborhood which they have selected for their own lies between Bleecker and Twelfth streets,
First avenue and East River.   The thoroughfares included within
these limits abound in tenement houses, and whole blocks of
them, especially in First, Second, Third, Fourth and Fifth streets
are inhabited exclusively by Bohemian families from garret to cel-
lar.   Within these limits may be found nearly all the Bohemians
in the city, excepting a few families which recently migrated up
town and established branch settlements in East Fifty-fourth and
East Eighty-second streets.   The writer was told by one who lives
among these people and knows them well, that it is a very rare
occurrence for one of them to live at any distance from the rest of
the colony, and that even those who moved up town make regular
and frequent visits to the parent settlement.
        A very large proportion of the Bohemians are engaged in
cigar-making others, are tailors, shoe-makers, artisans and saloon-
keepers, and, almost without exception, they belong to the work-

ing classes. Among themselves they speak their own peculiarly musical language, and in the neighborhood where they live Bohemian is the only language heard on the streets or seen on the shop sign-boards. They are organized into numerous benevolent, musical and social societies, exact copies of those which make up a large part of the life among the working classes in their own country. Prominent among these is a club composed exclusively of women, and established for the purpose of mutual relief and assistance in time of illness or other distress. This club numbers some three hundred members, and at the rooms, on Fourth street, where the meetings are held, there are displayed banners and insignia bearing mystic signs and evidently unpronounceable Bohemian mottoes, and a large frame containing the portraits of about one hundred of the most prominent women in the society. A dramatic society gives periodical and invariably well attended performances in the Bohemian language at one or another of the halls which abound in the Bohemian quarter.

The lager-beer saloon, as such, does not exist among the Bohemians, but the *Cesky Hostinec*, or Bohemian tavern, takes its place and fulfills all its functions and more. There is at least one *Cesky Host'nec* to every three tenement-houses in the Bohemian quarter; it serves not only as a beer-shop, but also as a reading-room, a resort for its patrons after working hours, and answers all the purposes of a cafe and club. Here any night one may meet the Bohemian in his true element, his long pipe in his mouth, his foaming glass of 'beer by his side, and occasionally his newspaper in front of him. Here, too, sometimes, and especially on Saturday nights, the women drop in for their weekly recreation, interchange of greetings, and the payment of the weekly bill; for the *Cesky Hostinec*, for the purpose of retaining its steady custom, gives a week's credit. Every customer is provided with a little book, which he sends to the place with every order, the order is entered in the book, and at the end of the week the account is made up and paid. The *Cesky Hostin'c* is used also as the meeting-room of the innumerable Bohemian societies, and in most of these tabernacles are to be seen, hanging on the walls, calls, notices, &c., in the Bohemian language, and banners, flags and other insignia. The most noticeable of these places are those of Nepivoda, at 152 Fourth street; Huback, at 533 Fifth street; Stocek, at 232 Third street; and the headquarters of the up-town branch colony, namely, the *Hostinec*, of Peter Stastny, at 320 East Fifty-fourth street.

The Bohemians do not read American papers, nor, as a rule,

German papers. They have a daily published in their own language, viz., the *Delnicke Listy*, or working-men's paper, which
describes itself as "the organ of the Socialist Working-men's Sec-
tion in the United States." This title tells at once the character
of the paper, and indicates the opinions held by its subscribers
and readers. Its columns contain, besides the current news of
the day, editorials on Bohemian politics, on the excise question
and on the labor troubles. It prints the platform adopted recently
by the Social Working-man's party at Newark, a list of all the Bohemian societies, orders and lodges, and other matters of interest
exclusively to the Bohemians. The *Delnicke Lis'y* is found in
every *Hostinec*, and is read by all the dwellers in the Bohemian
quarter.

The writer recently made a tour of this quarter and spent
much time in the various taverns and other resorts in conversation
with the frequenters of those places. For the most part they are
very intelligent and court. ous people, communicative and interesting, and, in appearance, not unlike the average German working-
man, except for a tendency that they have to grow long "impe-
rials." A majority of them, according to the statements of the
proprietors of the taverns mentioned and judging from their own
conversation, hold Socialistic views and a large number belong,
nominally at least, to the Socialist Working-Man's party.

One of the most intelligent and respectable Bohemians whom
the writer met said, in course of conversation about labor matters
in America: "I suppose we are very much like other working-
men; we want to be fairly paid for fair work, and, as the present
system does not give us fair pay or even assure us steady work,
we must try some other when we can. We, who know what the
oppression of aristocracies has done in Europe, are very determined not to give aristocracies any more show in America than
we can help. Yet you know that the rich here are rich enough to
be aristocrats, and the working-men are getting to be worse off
every day."

"Yes," interrupted a young man who sat at the next table,
"look at the cigar-makers. We have got a skilled trade and a hard
one; the bosses are rich; you never hear of a cigar firm failing,
and yet they are always shaving our wages"—

"It is not the shaving of wages," added the first speaker; it is
not that so much—the system is wrong. As long as the bosses
can get men to work for little or nothing they will do it. They
must be prevented from having the power to do it. We must
force the bosses to consult with their men about prices."

"Yes," put in the cigar-maker, "and if they wont they must

be made to. We have got wives and children as well as those fellows."

"But," suggested the writer, "do you not seek aid through politics to amend the laws?"

"Oh politics!" exclaimed the two Bohemians, in derision.

"What has politics to do with the working-man," asked the first speaker, "except to tax him with licenses and other things, and tell him he shall not drink beer when he wants it most? Why, that is the working-man's worst enemy. Politics is taking from us in taxes the little money that the bosses pay us. I ask my landlord to reduce my rent, and he says the taxes are too heavy. I complain that meat and clothes are too dear, and the butcher and clothier say the taxes are so heavy. I tell my boss he must pay me more wages, and he says business is bad and the taxes are heavy! To the devil with politics, say I!"

"Yes, and to the devil with politicians, I say!" added the cigar-maker.

"But how will Socialism help us in these troubles?" asked the writer.

"If Socialism or anything else will enable us to tax the men who can afford to be taxed, and let alone the working-man who cannot make enough to live, it will help us," was the reply.

The general conversation in the Bohemian colony was in this tone. Everywhere was found a feeling of discontent and depression, and a sentiment of absolute hostility to politics and taxes. "What do we get; how do we benefit because this is a free republic?" asked one. "It costs more in taxes in a free republic than it does at home, and you get less for it." "One man cuts down our wages, and another man makes our taxes larger," said another; "what wonder that people are Socialists, and strike and strive for better things?"

A DUKE WHO KEEPS AN INN.

THE somewhat famous hotel and restaurant in Hoboken, opposite the ferry landing, called "The Duke's House," is known by that name to most New Yorkers and to all Jerseymen. It has long been a place of resort for the better classes of Hoboken, and has been the scene of many an enjoyable dinner given by wealthy *gourmets* of other cities, and especially by some foreign residents of New York. Its proprietor, a ta l, handsome and elderly foreigner, is one of the characters of the place, and, partly because of his distinguished appearance and partly because few people know his name, he is almost universally called "The Duke." He responds to the title, and not only his customers but the servants in his employ use it. Few of the people who thus address him have any idea that he really has an indisputable right to the title, that he is in fact a re l duke and a member of one of the oldest and noblest families of Italy. He is the Duke of Calabritti.

Twenty-five years ago the Duke of Calabritti was one of the foremost noblemen of Italy and the leader of the *jeunesse doree* of Naples. Young, handsome and very wealthy, related to the oldest and noblest families of Southern Italy, the owner of the famous old Palazzo Calabritti. and the villas, farms and lands of great value, he was feted, courted and envied. He was given to gam ng, but as he played well and was rich enough to meet all his losses this did not at first affect his position. He was a favorite in Neapolitan society, and for a time a very king among men. His great physical beauty and his fastidious dress earned for him the name of "The Beau Brummel of Naples."

While still young the Duke of Calabritti contracted a marriage with an English lady, the daughter of a wealthy London gentleman. The match was not viewed with favor by his family, of the house of Pignatell, and wrought dismay among the matchmaking mothers, und the hopeful daughters of Neapolitan society. But the Duke was satisfied. After a tour of the Continent he brought his bride home and installed her in the historic palace which bears his name, and tor a few months lived in married happiness. About this time, however, he began to have very bad luck at the gaming table, losing largely and steadily. First his ready money went, and then he borrowed and still lost. One after the other his estates fell into the hands of the money-lenders until he became a comparatively poor man, and a positively poor nobleman. He then discovered, for the first time, that he had been the victim of a conspiracy on the part of a number of notorious blacklegs. It was too late, however, to repair the losses he had sustained, and his robbers had escaped with their spoils, His family, angry at the disgrace brought upon their home, had an open breach with the Duke, and he determined to leave the country.

He went to Paris, where he lived for some months, and afterwards to Brussels and the Netherlands. Tired of wandering about, he determined to settle in London, and was for some time a lion in the clubs and salons of that city. He was still a gambler, and frequently played, with varying fortune, for high stakes. Playing one night at the house of a well-known English nobleman, he had a serious difficulty with one of his opponents. Just as every one had begun to forget the affair, it was recalled by the act of the Duke of Calabritti himself. In some way the name of a woman became mixed up with it, and the Duke in a fit of anger revenged himself upon his enemy by an act which brought him into serious trouble. But for the timely aid of a friend, he would doubtless have been disagreeably dealt with. The Prince of Carrini. at the time Neapolitan Ambassador in London, interested himself in the Duke's behalf, and succeeded in getting permission for him to leave the country. The Duke accepted the terms, and determined to come to America.

Meanwhile the Duke's relations with his wife had become unpleasant. Influenced by her family, she refused to accompany him in his enforced emigration, and he accordingly left her behind. With her dowry, which had been settled upon her before her marriage, she had ample means, and, shortly after her husband's departure, she returned with her three children to Naples and took up her residence in the Palazzo Calabritti, where she has since lived in strict retirement.

The Duke came from London to New York in 1858 and lived for a time at the Astor House somewhat splendidly. He was accompanied by a beautiful Parisian girl, who was generally supposed to be the Duchess of Calabritti. After a few months of his sojourn here the Duke's money began to be exhausted, and, unable longer to support the expenses he was incurring, he determined to go South. The Parisienne remained in the city and opened a millinery store, sending her business cards around to people who had entertained her at their homes, and thereby created a social sensation which lasted for some time and which is probably not yet altogether forgotten.

The Duke next went to New Orleans, and after a sojourn of a four weeks there travelled incognito to South America, seeing the sights of that continent, and occasionally, of course, gambling. He was everywhere well received, and made many friends. After a tour of several months he returned about 1860 to New York, and determined to settle down here. His eyes fell upon the quiet, out-of-the way settlement of Hoboken, where he thought he would not be disturbed. His plan was to engage in some business which would get him a living, somewhere far enough away from temptation to enable him to keep a promise he had made to himself to give up gaming forever.

He accordingly opened a little bar-room and restaurant near the ferry, and kept it so skillfully, and devoted himself so entirely to the entertainment of his guests that it became very prosperous, and he made money. About eight years ago he built his present house, which has become celebrated for its excellent French and Italian dinners, for its choice wines, and, above all, for its macaroni, in the cooking of which the Duke is an adept. He goes to the market himself every morning, accompanied by his servant, and selects his own meat, game and vegetables. As a rule, he superintends only the general arrangements of the house; but, on special occasions, when distinguished gentlemen are his guests, he not only cooks the macaroni himself, but also waits on the table. On such an occasion one day there chanced to be present a young Italian nobleman, Nicolo Caraffa-Policastro, Duke of Forli, who was making a pleasure-trip in the United States. The families of Caraffa and Pignatelli had been very intimate in old times in Naples, and when the Duke of Forli was a boy the Duke of Calabritti, then in his prime was a visitor at the Palazzo Policastro. As soon as the elder Duke saw the younger Duke sit down at the table he eyed him anxiously, and during the whole dinner he never took his eyes off him. When the dessert was brought the Duke of Forli looked up and his eyes met those of the landlord and waiter.

' I beg your pardon," exclaimed the Duke of Calabritti, trembling and pale, ''but are you not from Naples?"

' Yes,' replied the Duke, looking perplexed.

"Is not your name Nicolo Caraffa-Policastro?" asked Calabritti again.

"Yes," said the other, and suddenly recognizing his questioner, ''You are the Duke of Calabritti!"

In a minute the two men were in each other's arms, Calabritti exclaiming, with the tears rolling down his cheeks, ''My Nicolino, my Nicolino, I have had you on my knee before you could talk my Nicolino.'

Only one man in the party had known who Calabritti was,

The others were at once let into the secret, and promised not to divulge it. For the Duke is not at all anxious to make his high rank known. To most of his acquaintances he is simply a very mysterious and courteous gentleman who pays his bills promptly and never refuses to do an act of charity when asked, a man who is evidently superior to his calling, but who is not disposed to divulge his affairs and will brook no questioning. To those who know him he says, "I like America and I like to live here. Being here, I, of course, want to do like the Americans and make my own living. I choose this business because in it I am always sure of two things which, on the whole, are essential to life—a good dinner and a bottle of good wine. If I get tired of this, which is very unlikely, I may go back to Italy, but at present I am very well satisfied and feel altogether contented."

In the Duke's household in Hoboken is an old gentleman of very distinguished appearance and very reserved manner, who came with him here from Italy. He lives quietly, rarely talks to any one, dresses well, and seems to have no occupation. Gossips say that the mysterious gentleman is a relative of the Duke, but those who claim to know say that he is an old family servant of the house of Pignatelli, who alone was true to his master, and whom he has most kindly and honorably declared shall be taken care of as long as he lives.

The Palazzo Calabritti, where the Duke was born, where he spent the most eventful years of his life, and where his wife and the future Duke of Calabritti still live, is well-known as one of the handsomest buildings in Naples. It stands at the entrance of the Chiaja, and makes a strong contrast to the comfortable little Hoboken hotel, known as the "Duke's House."

A MONKEYS' FINISHING SCHOOL.

MONKEYS are not born ready educated any more than men and women. They require to be taught, and are obliged to study hard before they reach that high state of development in which they are frequently found in circuses, at side-shows, on street-organs and in the other walks of monkey-life. In their primitive condition monkeys are not at all more intelligent than babies, but they have much more aptitude for acquiring knowledge, and are more amenable to discipline than the young ones of the human race. A large number of monkeys are educated in

New York, whence they are sent to delight the hearts of small
boys and sight-seers all over the country. Unfortunately they
have not the advantages that human beings have; their early surroundings are the reverse of respectable, and their instructors are
generally men and boys who have failed to distinguish themselves
in other and higher avocations. A few weeks ago, I visited "a
young monkeys' finishing school," situated on Baxter street, near
Worth. On arriving at No. 18, I inquired of an Italian fruit-vender
the way to the institution, and was led through an alley strewn
with garbage, dust, and old rags, up the rickety staircase of a two-
story hut in the rear, into a room about 10 feet by 8, in which
were three men, two boys, two half naked children, a large dog, a
small monkey, two bedsteads, a barrel of rotten fruit, and an ex-
United States soldier waiting with his organ, which was in need
of repairs. The windows, the panes of which were composed in
equal parts of glass, paper, rags and shoes, looked out upon a
back-yard in which was hung an abundance of linen recently
washed, but, judging from the appearance of the men in the neighborhood, not for the in-dwellers of the house. The proprietor of
the establishment, an old and almost blind Italian who, although
he has for years been travelling about in the country educating
monkeys in New Orleans and California, cannot speak a word of
English, introduced himself. He expatiated in terms of warm
praise, bad French and worse Italian, on the peculiar characteristics of the monkey and the unfailing effect of his method of in-
struction.

The monkey was then taken out of his box, and the old Italian having picked up the two children and chucked them into a
corner, and rolled the barrel of rotten fruit over to keep them
company, a space was cleared for his performance. The animal
began, of his own accord by standing on his head, turning a
somersault and pulling my walking-stick out of my hand. But
the professor seemed to reprehend this unprovoked activity, and
his pupil was promptly brought to order by the sight of a stout
riding-whip. Then, all being in order, the monkey went through
military movements with a gun, stood on his head, danced a
hornpipe, and, after much persuasion with the stock of the gun,
walked the length of the room on his forelegs. The company
then adjourned to the back yard aforementioned, where the dog
was saddled, and the monkey mounted him and rode round the
place in the most manly style.

The professor said it had taken him nearly six months to
teach the monkey the tricks he knew, and he did not consider
him perfect yet. Nevertheless, he would sell him to a circus for

$300. He had got him from an importer of monkeys, who had brought him from Africa. He had recently sold several little black monkeys, Capuchins he called them, at prices ranging from $70 to $150, according to the number of tricks they could perform; he charged so much for each monkey, and so much extra for each trick. He did not think there was any profit in selling one monkey at a time; he makes most by selling several together. He gets most of his animals from the importers; those which are tractable he trains for shows, circuses and organs, and those which are not tractable he sells to the Park Commissioners for exhibition in Central Park.

Continuing my tour around Baxter street, I learned that there was scarcely one Italian peanut merchant or ragpicker who had not at least one monkey for sale. Some of them go about with their pets concealed on their persons, always ready to produce them when there seems to be a prospect of a trade. Others leave them at home, spending their leisure hours in training them in the hope that they will eventually bring a good price. Among these men the monkey has a reputation for gentleness of disposition and docility of character which is hardly borne out by the manner in which they treat them. The monkeys all seem to understand Italian, French and English equally well, and the sad cast of their countenances apparently shows that, with them at least, a talent for modern languages is a matter of life and death.

The largest dealer in monkeys in the city is a man in Chatham street, near the Bowery. He buys his animals direct from the importer, and has a stock on hand, including specimens of the Capuchin, a native of Guinea, the Cacajo, of South Africa, the ape, the gorilla, the baboon and the chimpanzee. They range in price from $15 for a baby monkey, to $1,500 for a large, full-grown baboon. They are all uneducated, and have yet to be trained before they can be of much use to the circuses and side-showmen for whom they are intended. The Chatham street dealer sells a large number of small monkeys to people who make pets of them. Old maids and eccentric bachelors have a predilection for this class of domestic toys. The monkey is, strange to say, rather delicately constituted, and some of the race, particularly the variegated monkey with chestnut body, yellow head, yellow cheeks and black limbs, and the green monkey, with black face, are never seen in this country, because they cannot live outside of their own climate. The colored monkeys seen here are not the genuine article, and are usually got up to order, in the fashion of Mr. Barnum's woolly horse.

AMATEUR ACTORS.

SOCIETY is continually seeking new toys. Its latest play things are amateur dramatic societies and private reading clubs. Not that either of these institutions is absolutely novel, but they have never existed in such large numbers nor enjoyed such general popularity as now. It matters little whether this fact is due to an increased desire on the part of young people for literary recreation and mental self-improvement, or whether—which is a great deal more likely—it is due to the hard times and consequent scarcity of balls, parties and receptions, which renders it necessary for society folk to seek some new way of killing time. Certain it is that these institutions are growing apace, and no well-regulated young person can afford to disregard the prevailing fashion which requires the joining of one or the other or both. The amateur dramatic societies and reading clubs up-town are numbered by hundreds. Hardly a block of brown stone fronts from Twenty-third street to Harlem but has its society. They are so inexpensive, unostentatious, æsthetic and ostensibly innocent that papas and mammas greet their formation with satisfaction and yield a ready consent to their daughters' joining them. Innocent old folk! They little imagine that these clubs are simply the seeds of dances, hops, parties, and suppers which are, in the long run, destined to be far more expensive than the same number of regular balls would be.

Amateur dramatic societies, being the more pretentious of the two kinds of clubs alluded to, come first in order for consideration. They are composed usually of twenty or thirty young ladies and gentlemen, with an occasional sprinkling of stage-struck married people. It is by no means essential that the members should posess any histrionic ability. On the contrary, in many cases, absence of talent in this respect is rather a recommendation, as it puts all upon an equal footing, and obviates, to some extent, the danger of jealousy and rivalry. The organization of these societies is free of expense. The damages are, so to speak, indirect, coming in the form of bills for costumes and stage appointments, the former being defrayed by the actors and actresses, and the latter by assessments upon the gentlemen members. The performances are given at the residences of the lady members, each of whom plays hostess in her turn. And it is here that the expense to papa and mamma comes in. After the play is over, and the tragedy has been transformed into a comedy, or the comedy has been metamorphosed into a tragedy, as the case may be, of course the young folks dance, and of course the old folks provide the supper and ultimately pay, at least for the ladies' costumes, and so are wheedled, unknowingly, and in spite of themselves, into giving what is to all intents and purposes a regular party.

The amateur dramatic society-man is not the most modest of his race. He aspires to be a great actor. The old-fashioned parlor comedies, which his grandfather played in, do not satisfy the fire of ambition which burns within him. He dubs his society the "Booth," the "Wallack," the "Thespian," the "Barret" or the "Salvini," and goes in for the heaviest of comedy, the lightest of tragedy. He plays Claude Melnotte and his sweetheart plays Pauline, or he practices the *lex talionis* and murders Macbeth, while the least unobtrusive of the lady members makes short work of that monarch's wife. Any play in which there is plenty to say and little to do will suit. The amateur actor is generally pretty good at talking, but, somehow, or other, as soon as the table-cloth, which does service for a curtain, rises and discovers him on the floor of the back parlor, which passes for a stage he loses all control over his muscles and is strangely unable to use his limbs. He is all right in the rehearsals, but on the awful night of the performance he is otherwise. He usually complains of the chilliness of the room and fears an attack of the dumb-ague; he walks furiously up and down behind the scenes and bids the prompter be careful to speak loudly and distinctly. He is in mortal agony lest his mustache fall off, he is afraid his wig is awry, his boots are so tight he cannot walk, and he has no pockets in his clothes and does not know what on earth to do with his hands. He is mumbling to himself all the time the other *drama is personæ* are speaking, and is careful never to look at the person he is addressing, consistently and conscientiously staring at the blank wall, right over the head of the audience, while he is delivering his lines. Ten to one he is cast for the lover of the girl he does not care a pin for, while his hated rival is playing the lover to the girl he adores, or he is disconcerted by the sight of a man in the audience who has played his part and who grins when he blunders in his lines; in fact, there is no end to the sad possibilities of dire disaster which befall the amateur actor on his road to fame in private theatricals.

The young lady is more at home. She don't care whether she knows her lines or not, for nobody can hear her in either case. She always takes care to speak in a whisper, quite inaudible two feet from the stage, and to this extent she is safe. She is usually more thoughtful of her dress and its claims to the notice

of the audience than she is of her part in the play. She, too, is
all right at rehearsal, but, when the night of the playing comes on
she is apt to forget her cue, and keep the audience and actors
waiting a minute or two in dead silence while she gives a last
touch to her dress and takes a last look in the glass.   Then she
enters, radiant, beautiful, just on the point of taking up the
thread of the dialogue quite forgotten by the audience, when a
burst of applause greets her, disconcerts her, and she stands silent and bathed in—rouge, until the voice of the prompter, heard
loud above all the applause, spurs her into action again.   No
matter what may be the exigency of the dramatic situation she
will allow no unusual familiarities, not even the semblance of a
kiss, nor the shadow of an embrace. She will wear modern jewelry, no matter now ancient the time of the play, and has not the
remotest idea of the importance of small details in stage business.

The male amateur is always eminently satisfied with his own
dramatic and elocutionary powers, and scorns the extraneous aid
of professionals. Not so the female amateur, who takes lessons in elocution and deportment from Miss Fanny Morant, or
from the modest person who advertises in the daily papers, as follows :

AN accomplished actress and dramatic reader teaches elocution, prepares
   pupils for the stage, instructs and directs rehearsals; voice-building for
the pulpit, bar and stage; making the weakest voice smooth and powerful.
Address "LADY TEAZLE," Post-Office.

In time the female amateur becomes sublimely self-confident,
and indulges in wild dreams of appearing on the professional stage
and wearing dresses like unto those of Fanny Davenport. The
male amateur, on the other hand, looks down with sublime con-
descension upon the dramatic profession, and thinks he does it
honor when he deigns to play with it.

The height of ambition in the breast of the average amateur
actor is reached when he is allowed to appear in public for the
benefit of some charitable institution—and charity covers his sins,
among others. His appearance at the Union League or Terrace
Garden Theatre in the plays of "A Serious Family," "The Colleen
Bawn" or "The Hunchback" becomes a tradition in his family,
and he is never tired of describing his triumph and the fit of his
costume. On occasions of public performances, however, the
lady amateurs usually back out, their papas objecting to the un-
due publicity of the thing, and their places are filled by professional actresses who cannot get an engagement elsewhere. This
is no exaggeration, for, as everybody knows, there is no severer
test of the amiability, patience and long suffering of a reasonable
being than attendance at an amateur entertainment in aid of some

soup-kitchen or hospital. Having got your money for the tickets, and that money going to the charity to be benefited and not to them, the performers feel in no way called upon to consult your interests or to consider your feelings. They play to amuse themselves, and, if they have any sense of humor at all, their object must generally be attained. The more pretentious of the regularly organized dramatic societies are constantly on the lookout for opportunities to appear in public and to hide their ambition under the mantle of charity. They are a perennial source of annoyance to the better class of benevolent associations, whose clerks are kept busy answering and declining offers of performances and subsequent select receptions for their benefit. They are, at the same time, a mine of wealth to the smaller philanthropic institutions, for whose advantage they are permitted to operate upon the nerves of the charitably-disposed theatre-going public. The great liberality of amateur actors may be judged from an offer recently made to an association formed for the purpose of erecting a monument to a distinguished man, proposing to give a performance in aid of the monument-fund free—if it was given 200 tickets, half of all the boxes and $300 in cash for its expenses. The secretary added that this generous offer was made on behalf of the amateur association, whose members were anxious to aid in the monument project, but were not able to contribute in cash.

Closely allied to the amateur theatrical societies are the so-called reading clubs. These are composed of somewhat different material. They partake of the character of "sociables," and usually have about thirty or forty members, ladies and gentlemen, all more or less acquainted and moving in the same society. The club meets at the houses of the lady members, and winds up each entertainment with a dance and a supper. These features are, however, less pretentious than in the case of the amateur actors, who do not care to go to the trouble of studying, rehearsing and dressing, unless they are permitted to inflict their performances upon tolerably large assemblages. The members of the reading clubs have not the trouble of dressing, for swallow-tails and "low-necks" are forbidden; of course, they have no occasion to rehearse, and any one who attends a reading can easily see for himself that studying is altogether dispensed with. Four or five members are chosen to read at each meeting, and every person so chosen is free to select for himself or herself what "piece" he or she will perpetrate. So it is not an unfrequent occurrence for an evening's entertainment to consist of, say; "Enoch Arden," "Horatius," "Lord of Burleigh," "Shamus O'Brien" and "The Bells," or of "The Raven," "The Son of the Evening Star," "Sheridan's

Ride," "The Night Before Waterloo" and "Marc Antony's Ora-
ion." The members are, as a rule, eminently conservative in
their tastes, and never select any "piece" which is not "standard," or has not been read a thousand times before. They are
careful not to evince the least emotion while the readings are
going on, but preserve a death-like silence until their close, when
they appl in l all, equally, impartially and indiscriminately. The
most difficult selections are oftenest selected. Thus every young
man wants to have "The Bells," and every young lady is ambitious to tackle "The Lord of Burleigh.' The ladies display the
same talent for hiding their short-comings in reading-clubs that
they do on the amateur stage, and always read sotto voce, completely dropping their voices when they come to a difficult word.
The gentlemen, on the other hand, take the orthoepic vowel by
the horns, and shout louder than any others the words they cannot pronounce. A common pastime of reading-club people is to
select a well-known scene from a popular play, and rob it of its
proper charm. The quarrel scene between Sir Peter and Lady
Teazel in the "School for Scandal," and the love scene between
King Harry and the French Princess in "Henry the Fifth," are favorite subjects.

The theatrical itch has spread even to the reading-clubs, and
it is not an unfrequent thing for them to close their bi-montbly
meetings with charades which bear just enough resemblance to
priva e theatricals to be tolerable—no more—and to satisfy the
craving of modern younglidydom for an opportunity to disport
itself upon a floor bearing the semblance of a stage, clad in garments not unlike theatrical trappings, in a piece which might
under remotely conceivable circumstances, pass for a play.

A HORRIBLE TALE.

LAST Thursday evening, while Mr. Morris Wolf, of No. 586 Second Avenue, was seated at his door stoop, one Kiernan took forcible possession of his dog, a family pet, which was both muzzled and licensed. Mr. Wolf remonstrated, when Kiernan became exceedingly demonstrative and threatened to shoot the owner of the animal, besides being abusive. Appreciating the fact that he had a ruffian to deal with, an officer was called in, who promptly arrested the intruder, who, on being brought before Justice Morgan committed him.—Jewish paper.

And yet we call this a free country! Was such an outrage as this ever before perpetrated in the light of our boasted nineteenth century civilization? Was a Jewish journal ever before called upon to chronicle such a dastardly violation of the principles which underlie our social, political and religious institutions? Does not the Hilton infamy pale its ineffectual fires in the light of this latest and most atrocious villainy, happily exposed by the mighty power of that potent engine of public opinion—the press? But let us consider this horrible anomaly in a calm and judicial spirit.

Here we have it stated on apparently good authority that on a Thursday evening, of all evenings in the week, Mr. Morris Wolf was calmly and quietly seated "at his door stoop," and, as far as the evidence shows, he was the only Wolf at his door. By his side, in mute enjoyment of the picturesque scenery of Second Avenue, sat a family pet, his dog,—no common dog either, but one that was "both muzzled and licensed." What a charming scene of the simplicity of domestic human and canine life under the starry flag of the American Republic is here presented! But, stay! the serpent is on the trail, the calm of the midsummer evening scene on the east side is but the precursor of the storm to come. Suddenly there appears "one Kiernan,"—the veracious chronicler is conscientiously careful to inform us that there is only one of him—and seizes the family pet. He does not attempt to argue with the dog, he uses no powers of persuasion, no! not he, ruthless disturber of the domestic peace of the Wolf household; he takes the bull by the horns, or rather, the dog by the tail; he takes "forcible possession" of him and rudely bears him away.

Mr. Wolf, wounded in his tenderest feelings at this high-handed outrage upon his pet, very naturally remonstrates; but in vain, the tyrant's ears are deaf to all entreaties—and it never seems to have occurred to Mr. Wolf to try the effects of a five-dollar bill. Kiernan, instead of being melted to tears at the remonstrances of his victim, does—what?—why he actually has the au-

dacity to become demonstrative. We have the statement here in
black and white. More,—he threatens to shoot Mr. Wolf, thus
causing him to sacrifice his life for his dog; and, not content with
being demonstrative and threatening to shoot, he adds insult to
injury by "being abusive." Nor have we any information that
any of the witnesses of this diabolical deed raised their voices in
protest.

At this stage of the proceedings, having had his dog stolen,
having seen the thief become demonstrative," having heard him
threaten murder and having, finally, seen him "abusive" besides,
Mr. Wolf begins to take in the situation. He begins to "appreci-
ate the fact that he has a ruffian to deal with"—which shows that
Mr. Wolf is an appreciative man. What then? He calls in an
officer who "promptly arrested the intruder," and it really seemed
as though justice was about to triumph; but, alas! how little do
they know of that which is, who base their hasty judgment upon
that which seems! Kiernan is taken to court, but, instead of being punished, he has the audacity to reverse the order of things
by committing the magistrate. The reporter plainly says that
Kiernan "on being brought before Justice Morgan, committed
him." This was the crowning outrage. Where is our vaunted
American freedom, where is the sanctity of our laws, when a ras-
cally dog-catcher who is arrested and taken to court can sit in
judgment on his judge and commit him? Was such a thing
ever heard of before? If such a thing can ever occur again, had
we not better abolish our courts altogether, and bow down to the
sovereign rule of the dog-catcher?

But, the chapter of villainy is not yet complete. Because a
Jew was the victim in this case, no doubt, the daily papers mali-
ciously suppressed all mention of it, and, had it not been for our
enterprising, courageous and intelligent Jewish contemporary,
this outrage might never have seen the light of day, might have
been allowed to fester in darkness, corrupting every branch of our
city government, and sapping the very foundations of American
liberty. But the paper we quote is edited by an alderman of the
city of New York, who, in his official capacity, had to do with the
appointment of dog-catcher Kiernan. Certainly the alderman
will use his influence to have him removed, to right this crying
wrong, and to vindicate the majesty of our outraged laws. Such
villainous proceedings as these must be checked, or the day of
dire disaster is not far distant, when the people will rise up in
their might to demand justice, even though they have to reach it
through oceans of crimson gore!

THE MIDSUMMER MAIDEN.

THE midsummer maiden is a production, aged somewhere between 18 and 25, common to all civilized countries and abounding in the United States in large numbers. They are not exactly a product of nature, as nature furnishes only the raw material, leaving the maiden to complete herself according to her taste—if she has any. Nor can they be called altogether artistic, for the art they employ seldom serves to hide their deformities.

Of late the midsummer maiden has become quite popular among the admirers of curiosities, so that almost every American household has at least one. But it is on the hotel piazzas at summer (last) resorts, in the saloons and on the decks of our pleasure-boats, and in the cosy recesses of our drawing-room railroad cars that they are found in the greatest abundance.

Midsummer maidens are usually distinguished by their little feet, little hands, little waists and little minds. Sometimes they have no minds, but in such cases nature endows them with a wealth of tongue, and a development of cheek enough to make up for the deficiency—such is the law of compensation and the eternal fitness of things.

The average midsummer maiden is peculiarly constructed; when in a natural state she is sometimes a collection of sharp angles, superfluous elbows, shoulders and hipbones, with sometimes great scarcity of hair and impure complexion. But, when dressed up for business, she is graceful and elegant; she has a beautifully-rounded figure, luxurious growth of hair and a dazzling complexion. To acquire this valuable stock in trade, she undergoes a perfect martyrdom of tight-lacing, padding, squeezing and wrenching. She submits herself to the hands of the painter and decorator, and, such is her heroic devotion to her business and such her determination to succeed in it, that she actually does not hesitate to wear on her head the cast-off tresses of prison convicts, hospital patients, and morgue subjects, in the form of curls, chignons and puffs.

The chief business of the midsummer maiden is to change her condition—not, as some scientific writers have maintained, to improve it—for she often does the former without achieving the latter. She feels that she is in a transitory state, like the worm which is about to become a butterfly, only that she plays butterfly first; often, alas, to be trodden on as a worm hereafter. In one sense she is a worm before marriage; she is scoured and dried, and the jewelled hook is run through her ear and she is used as bait to catch gudgeon. In this way she is useful to papas in difficulties, with no assets but their daughters, these being usually willing to realize on themselves.

The arts used by the midsummer maidens to secure their game are various and peculiar, but they excite little wonder when we remember that the whole life of the species is devoted to this one object. From infancy upward, they are taught by the old ones of their kind to regard themselves as licensed, professional catchers, and the catching of men as legitimate and maidenly sport. Old women—old enough to know better—teach the maidens, even before they are able to talk, to "make eyes," to kiss, and "to flirt."

When the maidens are just about able to walk and talk—the latter comes to them by nature and stays—they are taught to go through certain gyratory movements, yclept dancing, so as to excite the interest, admiration, and warmer feelings of the men, and also to bring about the opportunities for engagements at closer quarters. As they grow older, great care is paid to their dress, and especially to shoes and stockings, which are of the most fantastic designs, and of which a suggestive inch or two is always visible.

Arrived at the age when they can go into business regularly, the M. M.'s are taught the use of certain powders, paints, cosmetics and unguents to make their skin pleasant to the sight and touch, and agreeable to the smell. They are also shown how to dress in such a way as to expose as much as possible such natural charms as they may have, while at the same time hiding such deformities as they may suffer from; so that the girl who is really handsome, when on business, wears very little dress at all.

Thus simply attired, she ambles into the open matrimonial mart, the ball-room, throws herself into the arms of the first man she knows, and he, clasping his arm around her waist, rushes up and down the room with her, like a madman goaded to frenzy by the sight of so much beauty undisguised, or as if determined to punish the girl by a sort of circular tread-mill action. Incidentally, he will sometimes tear off her back what little dress she has there; for, be it noted, the average M. M. usually wears two yards of dress on the ground for every one she wears on her person. This, however, is mainly in the ball-room, elsewhere she not infrequently wears a dress that covers her form, though even then she has it so cut as to reveal in suggestion, what it but half conceals in fact. Other arts she employs in the pursuit of her avocation are, playing with the piano, reciting poetry in a high key with musical accompaniment, the use of the fan as a weapon of offense and defense, especially the former, and the manœuvres of the handkerchief.

The M. M. is gregarious. In flocks she haunts the park, the bluff, the beach, the hotel piazzas and corridors; she is alike at home in all. No place comes amiss to her; where'er she be the can throw her line and play her fish. Summer hotel hops and straw rides were invented for her special benefit, and there are writers who maintain that moonlight evenings, with her inevitable "strolls," were also established for her advantage, but proof is lacking on this point.

Some people think it essential to a man's happiness to have at least one M. M. This is a sad mistake, and often leads to dire results, which are seen in the Divorce court records. Sometimes an M. M., if taken young, and tamed and carefully handled, will turn out a tolerable, and occasionally, even a good wife. But the vast majority of them are unable to shake off the effects of early evil habits, and remain M. M.'s to the death, for which they usually prepare their toilettes and decorations far in advance, so that they may enter the hereafter, armed with the same arts and wiles that they practised here.

"MY UNCLE."

IT appears from the last census that there were in 1870 only 384 pawnbrokers in the United States, but the actual number must be considerably greater. In New York there are eighty licensed pawnbrokers, who must be American citizens, must have resided in the city one year, and have paid $50 license and given bonds of $1,000 before they were accorded the privilege of conducting their business. There are, no doubt, many unlicensed pawnbrokers, and jewellers, and others who do a money-lending business *sub rosa*. Certainly many persons engaged in the business are averse to having their occupation known. Pawnbroking has of late years been considered somewhat disreputable, notwithstanding that the first pawnbrokers were Italian merchants from Lombardy, of high standing in their own country, and had noble and royal customers. Edward I, of England, pawned the customs of his kingdom for a heavy loan, and Edward III and Richard II pledged the crown jewels. In the sixteenth century the descendants of the Lombard pawnbrokers had become so overbearing and extertionate that they were expelled from France and England, and laws were enacted to deliver the poor from their extortions. Members of the famous Medici family were foremost among the money-lenders of the middle ages.

The pawnbrokers of the present day are no better than their predecessors, from whom they have inherited their cruel greed, as they maintain the trade-sign of three gold balls, derived from the armorial bearings of the ancient corporation of Lombards. But the recent enactments in regard to usury have somewhat curtailed the profits of the business. In thirty-three States and Territories, the regular rate of interest varies from six to twelve per cent. Iu California, Florida, Maine, Montana, Nevada, New Mexico, Rhode Island, South Carolina, Texas, Utah, Washington and Wyoming, all usury laws have been abolished, and any rate of interest agreed upon may be collected. New York has the most stringent usury laws; the maximum rate of interest is fixed at seven per cent., and violations of the law are made misdemeanors, punishable by fine, imprisonment and forfeiture of the principal. Nevertheless, exorbitant interest is invariably collected by round-about methods, contrived successfully to evade the law: The brokers charge for the ticket, charge for registering, charge for storage—anything to swell their profits.

The pawnbrokers of New York do business chiefly on the Bowery, Third, and Sixth avenues, and on the side streets between Bleecker and Fourteenth. They are most numerous in the poorest districts. There are no less than six of them on three blocks near the beginning of Sixth avenue. Just now, business is lively with them; the prevalent depression in all trades and industries has reduced so many, hitherto well-to-do people to absolute want, that the pawn-shops are overstocked with wearing apparel and household goods of all kinds, pledged not unfrequently to procure a much needed loaf of bread. The consequence is that the brokers are offering very limited loans, and many of them will not take in anything but jewelry, which is always marketable, and which, as it is seldom redeemed, is a source of much gain to them.

The articles most frequently pawned are watches and rings, on which the money lenders usually advance from one-half to two-thirds of their value. Clothing is taken in pledge only at the lower class of pawnshops, and, unless it is new, or almost new, very little money can be raised on it. All pledges are kept for one year, and at the end of that time those left unredeemed become the property of the broker, whose chief profit comes from this branch of his trade. It frequently happens that stolen goods are pawned by thieves or their agents, and pawnbrokers are consequently subject to frequent visits by the police in search of lost property. Nearly all of the so-called diamond-brokers on Broadway and side streets are pawnbrokers who surreptitiously buy all sorts of property, and advance money on all classes of valuables "and no questions asked." They are under strict police surveillance. The legal requirement that every person offering an article in pledge shall give his or her name and address is practically useless, as about eighty-four per cent. of people so pledging give assumed names and false addresses.

The scenes and incidents of pawnbrokers' shops have been so often, and so graphically described, that it is not necessary to treat of them here. As a rule the shops are well kept and orderly, and whatever grief or trouble may penetrate there does not disturb the peace. The sight of men pledging their tools, and women their household utensils, for money wherewith to buy intoxicating drinks, which is so terribly common in England, is happily rare among us. On the other hand, people of very fair social position, who, in England, would not dare to enter a pawnshop, frequent such places here whenever the necessity arises.

Professional gamblers are perhaps the pawnbroker's best customers. They generally wear an abundance of jewelry, and, when bad luck sets in, they part with their baubles, one by one, to raise the means to "get square" again. A large number of wedding rings are pawned every year, and more of them are redeemed than of any other kind of jewelry. The wedding ring is usually the last trinket with which a woman will part, and if it goes 'tis probably to restore a dying child to life, or to feed a famishing family. So many watches have been pawned of late, that the brokers will now advance on them only the value of the metal unless the watch be of a celebrated make. The consequence of this is, that watches are cheaper than ever, and can be bought in running order as low as $2. It is very common for people to take imitation gold to the pawnbroker's in the hope that it may pass for genuine, but the hope is always delusive. The money-lender is too much an adept at getting the better of others ever to allow anyone to get the better of him. He is always provided with a bottle of strong acid and a pair of scales, and can tell to a fraction the exact value of every piece of metal offered to him.

Pawnbrokers, more than any other class of men, except sheriffs' officers, profit by the misfortunes of their neighbors. As one of them said the other day to the writer: "Hard times or good times don't make no matter of difference to us; there is always folks wanting money and ready to get it the best way they can."

ON Sunday morning an unknown man was found by the police of the Nineteenth Precinct dying in the street. He was taken to the station-house and died on the way there. The coroner's inquest showed that death had resulted from natural causes, and the body was taken to the Morgue. On Tuesday the dead man was identified and proved to be Herman Christopher Schnobel, a native of Libau, Russia, aged sixty-five, and the father of two girls, aged respectively fifteen and seventeen, who live with Mrs F. M., of East Fifty-sixth street. From Mrs. M. and Schnobel's daughters, it appears that he was at one time a wealthy, and highly respected merchant in his own country and a member of a very good family. According to their story, moreover, corroborated by letters, papers and certificates examined by the writer, he appears to have had an eventful and somewhat romantic life.

Some twenty years ago, then a middle-aged man and a bachelor, he was a prosperous merchant in the town of Libau, where his brothers, Edward Schnobel, at one time a Russian Consul in Italy, and Dr. Carl Schnobel, still reside. He was a man of lively temperament, fond of pleasure, and welcome in the best society. He formed the acquaintance of a handsome and fascinating actress, by name Antonis, reputed to be the illegitimate daughter of a wealthy nobleman; fell in love with her, and against the wishes of his family and friends she became his wife. His relatives, displeased at what they regarded as his marriage beneath his station, disowned him and refused to recognize him. Schnobel, nevertheless, remained true to his wife, and for four or five years they lived very happily together. She bore him two children, the present wards of Mrs. M. Not more than a year after the birth of her second child Mrs. Schnobel became acquainted with an officer in the Russian army. They fell in love. They decided to elope, and, leaving her husband and children without a word, Mrs. Schnobel gathered up all the jewelry and money she could find, and fled with her lover to America. Poor Schnobel was nearly heartbroken. He began to neglect his business, his health failed, and after five years of weary searching for his lost wife, hearing that she was in America, he determined to follow her. Here he came, with the few thousand roubles he had saved from his ruined business, about ten years ago.

Arriving in New York he embarked in business, and founded the house of Schnobel & Co., commission merchants in fancy goods, at 81 New Canal street. He did fairly well for a time, and about four years ago he sent to Russia for his daughters, whom he had left in care of some friends. In 1875, owing to some cause not clearly explained, Schnobel suddenly failed, and found himself bankrupt and almost penniless. All this time he had been inquiring for his lost wife, but had been able to discover nothing of her. Thrown on the world at sixty-three, with two children to support, he tried hard to find employment, but in vain. Though he was well-educated and could speak five languages, he could not earn the price of a meal. His little stock of money was almost gone, when Mrs. M., who had known him in his better days, offered to take his eldest girl to her home and care for her. The offer was thankfully accepted, and later, as his prospects grew worse and worse, she took charge of the second daughter also.

For the past two years Schnobel had been living from hand to mouth, as best he could, his children giving him such help as they could afford. On Saturday last the keeper of the house in West Thirteenth street, where he lodged, called and informed them that their father was missing. They made all possible inquiries, and on Monday they went the Morgue, but were refused admission by the keeper. On Tuesday they saw their father's death announced in the paper, and went to Coroner Croker, who gave them a permit to visit the Morgue, and there they found the dead body of the missing man. That was all they could do; they had no money to pay for a decent funeral, and, kissing the cold face of their father, they left him there to be buried in the Potter's Field. "But," said the younger girl to the writer, "we shall write to our relatives in Russia for money, and then, when it comes, the gentleman at the Morgue says he will give us our papa, and we can bury him properly." The girls have written to Russia in this hope.

Among Schnobel's papers were the baptismal certificates of his children, his passport, certificates of his decoration by the Emperor with orders-of-merit for distinguished services in the army, and several letters, all written in German. There were also some letters from his wife, of whom little is known. She and her husband never met after her elopement. Mrs. M. says that the companion of her flight died about five years ago, and that, shortly after, Mrs. Schnobel went to Milwaukee, and has not been heard of since.

IN THE EDITOR'S SANCTUM.

THE modern daily newspaper, and particularly the modern American daily newspaper, is a puzzle to most people. Except to those who are familiar with the inside workings of the great offices, the mysteries of the profession are positively bewildering. But there are a few points about it which may be explained. Reference is made in particular to the news and editorial departments.

To begin with, every newspaper has a chief editor, a Raymond, a Bennett, or a Greeley, who directs its general policy, dictates the tone of its editorals, and exercises a general supervision of its interests. Next to him in rank is the managing editor, who controls the news columns, and acts as the chief's first lieutenant, in carrying out the objects of the journal. The city-editor has charge of all matters occurring in the city, and is the commander-in-chief of a small army of reporters. These are the three chief functionaries. Besides them, to say nothing of the editorial writers, there are, a dramatic critic, a financial editor, and others in charge of the commercial, real estate, live-stock, and foreign departments of the paper, each being supreme in his special line, and subject only to the orders of the managing editor. This last, named functionary is really the most important man in the office, for, in most offices, the chief is rarely seen, and issues his orders usually by proxy.

The managing editor's chief assistant is the night-editor , who has charge of the arrangement of the matter in the paper, edits all the out-of-town copy that comes into the office during the evening, writes the heads to telegraphic despatches and correspondence, as the night city editor does to the local matter, and takes the manager's place after he leaves the office. The night-editor is responsible for having the paper printed in time for the early mails and newsmen, for getting in all matter of pressing importance, and for seeing that nothing of an objectionable character is printed after the managing editor leaves. It will thus be seen that his position is by no means easy or even agreeable.

Another assistant of the manager is the day-editor, who generally has charge of the correspondence—a very important department on a large paper—and represents the manager when he is absent from the office during the day. He is also the unhappy being who receives and listens to the thousand and one bores who infest newspaper offices, and rush to them to tell their private grievances, or their supposed public wrongs. He is compelled to sympathize with the woes of one and the ambitions of another. Often he has to exercise that patience, which is characteristic of newspaper-men, when he is approached by the belligerent caller who comes to get an apology or "clean out the office." He is the unhappy being on whom amateur poets draw their manuscripts and to whom literary young ladies look for aid, comfort and advice.

Not at all the least important persons on a great daily paper are the reporters. They may be divided into two general classes: first, the routine workers, such as those who report meetings of public boards and societies, the doings at police headquarters, at the City Hall, and in the courts; secondly, the descriptive writers who do up public ceremonies and exhibitions, write fancy sketches, and do the light work generally. A peculiar class of reporters, who cannot be included in either category, are those employed to do detective work, ferret out political and other secrets, interview public and private persons, and do work, generally of such a character that, while it is a necessary element of lively and enterprising journalism, the editors who direct it to be done would, under no circumstances, take a hand in it themselves.

Other important newspaper people are the regular correspondents, not the amateur correspondents who write special letters on special occasions, but the staff-men who do the drudgery and labor at Washington. or at Albany during the legislative sessions, keep their papers supplied with news, and keep their eyes on the public servants, ever ready to detect and expose a job or a theft. To these men the people owe the revelations of official corruption which are made from time to time; of these men the dishonest or incompetent official is more afraid than of the whole government.

The travelling or special correspondents, who journey from place to place to describe a fire, an explosion, or a flood, or keep the people informed upon political prospects in times of election, are also very important members of the profession, and are frequently charged with very delicate and responsible functions.

So much, in brief, for the men of the newspapers, or rather the chief men (for many less indispensible personages are necessarily omitted, such as the resident foreign correspondent, summer-resort correspondent, and occasional contributor.) Now a word as to how they do their combined work.

The contents of a great newspaper may be divided under three heads: the editorial, news and advertising departments. The first is in charge of the chief editor, the second, of the managing editor, and the third, of the publisher or his representative in the publication office. The editorials, political and other, are, with few exceptions, written by the regular paid staff writers, who sometimes choose their own subjects, and are sometimes assigned their topics, the articles in every case being approved by the chief editor before their publication. Some of them are written leisurely and at great pains; others, and by far the majority, are dashed off hurriedly late at night to accompany the news on which they are based. This has been the case with some of the most brilliant and vigorous newspaper writing ever printed.

The news comes from various sources. Foreign and domestic correspondence and special city articles often come to the office in the daytime. These the day-editor or city-editor makes ready for the prin'ers, who begin setting them in type at seven in the evening. Most of the city news, however, comes from the reporters late at night, and is hurriedly read and revised and sent to the printers. The domestic and foreign despatches come at all hours of the night, from special and regular correspondents, and from the two great news-channels, the Associated Press and the National Press Association. These companies have agents all over the world, who send to the central office in New York accounts of everything of interest occurring in their respective localities. As fast as the press despatches reach the newspaper offices they are turned over to the night-editor and his assistants, who revise and summarize them, write the head-lines and communicate the chief topics of interest to the editorial writers, who make the editorial comments. Perhaps not more than one-half of all the matter sent over the wires is ever seen in print. It is cut and boiled down, altered and condensed, and put into shape to fit the available space, which varies according to the number and importance of local and other events. Frequently long despatches, reporting startling events at distant points, reach the office very late at nigh:, or perhaps just a few minutes before the hour of going to press, which is usually two A. M., and the night-editor and his assistants have to handle them skilfully and rapidly to get the news into the paper in some form. Failing this, a second, and if necessary, a third extra edition is issued.

Besides the press associations already mentioned there are local companies, such as the City and Metropolitan Press Associations, which supply the papers with such local matter as their reporters may fail to obtain, or which is worth using but not worth sending for. The matter coming from these sources passes through the city-editor's hands, and is treated in the same way as the other press matter. All these news associations are absolutely and necessarily non-political.

Usually the last "copy" which reaches the hands of the printers on a daily paper is the dramatic criticism, which, being written after the performances, is late in arriving at the office. Sometimes the critic goes there to write, but more frequently he goes to his club to do his work and sends his article down to the office.

On occasions of important public events the work done in American newspaper offices is really marvellous. Take, for example, election day. The polls close at four, on the afternoon of one day, and by two A. M. on the next morning, the papers are out with full returns from all over the country. This result is achieved only by great enterprise. The papers have special correspondents in every state capital, and telegraphic wires in their offices communicating with the centres of news all over the city, and the whole staff is busily at work all night in figuring up the results. Sometimes there are thirty or forty men at work at the same time, without counting the editorial writers, who are busily engaged in crowing over victories or condoling with their party in defeat, as the case may be. To see the startling head-lines and "roosters," which appear on the following day at the heads of newspaper columns, one would suppose that the editor had spent the night in joyful carousings rather than in hard, exhausting work.

In enterprise, brightness, accuracy and public spirit, the newspapers of America are unequalled. They are true representatives of the people of the country. They are the daily food, as well as the chief educators, of the nation. One copy of the average first-class American journal contains more general information, more bright writing, more pathos, humor and wisdom than can be found in a whole volume of newspapers published in any other part of the world. Truly we may be proud of the American press. Its power is so wide and far-reaching that it would be surprising if it were not sometimes abused; but, taken as a whole, it is an institution of which more good than evil can be said and whose influence is most frequently exercised on the side of justice and enlightenment.

A BAVARIAN FEST TAG

MYRTLE Avenue Park is a rural spot in the furthermost part of East Brooklyn, on the avenue from which it takes its name. It is not much of a park, hardly a match in size for Jones's Wood, and in natural beauty it is not much ahead of Tompkins Square, in its present condition. Indeed, except for a few leafless trees and occasional patches of parched grass, it has none of the features of a park at all. Nevertheless, it proved to be a very attractive resort yesterday on the occasion of the annual volkfest of the Bavarian societies of Brooklyn, which took place there, and drew to the grounds several hundred people of Bavarian birth, or descent, and of all kinds and degrees. The park was decorated in honor of the event with the Bavarian and American national colors, and all around were scattered signs of rejoicing and festivity. Just inside the gates was a diminutive bowling-alley, a little further on, a dancing-platform with a rude bar, on which were two kegs of lager on tap at one end, and a stand for the coatless and spectacled musicians at the other. Near the dancing-floor was another platform on which were stacked a dozen or so of rifles, as if to protect the kegs of lager mounted on a box just behind them. Standing guard over the whole were two members of the Schutzenverein in full uniform, and around the stands was the legend, "Hauptquartier des Bayerisches Volkfest." Of course there was a merry-go-round, revolving to the music of a hand-organ and the joyous shouts of the youngsters, and there were the fruit-stand, ice-cream saloon, and lager-beer stations without number. The inevitable photograph gallery was present and doing a good business, as was the man with the machine to "try your muscle," and also the Punch-and-Judy show, and a "Grand Parisian Panorama of the Philadelphia Exposition," with a German drummer, who declared that the show had received the highest encomiums from Carl Schurz and President Hayes.

The scene presented was very similar to those witnessed at the periodical Kermesses in Brussels, Antwerp, and other Continental cities. The assemblage, too, was very much of the same character, consisting mainly of small retail dealers and clerks, with their wives and all their children. The large number of babies and small boys present was noticeable. Most of the guests arrived in family groups—the father, in his best broadcloth suit, carrying a small satchel with the day's provisions, and with one young one hanging to the skirts of his coat on either side; the mother with an infant of tender years in her arms, and some more young ones hanging to her skirts. One group consisted of a father and mother, each carrying one of the recently arrived twins, and five other small children besides.

"You have a large family here," suggested the writer, in German.

"Yes, fellow-countryman." was the reply; "but we can't make any discrimination, you know. Mother must come, and I must come, and so we have to bring the children. (Patronizingly)—would you like to hold one of the twins for a minute?"

The costumes of some of the worthy pic-nickers added much to the picturesqueness of the scene. A couple, apparently new arrivals from the Fatherland, were attired in the most approved Bavarian style. Madame had her head enveloped in a vari-colored silk handkerchief, from which her red face smiled pleasantly upon a plain-cut dress, of which the body was of bright red, and the skirt of red with a single border of purple. A green silk apron and a heavy gold chain completed the toilet. Meinherr was attired in a full suit of broadcloth, the jacket cut very short, just to the hips, and the trousers cut very wide, except at the ankles, where they were correspondingly narrow. A round black hat, such as is known in England as a "a pork-pie," a heavy watch-chain, and a large and snow-white shirt frill set off his handsome figure. There were many members of the Schutzenverein and Singerverein and of vereine of every description, all in their society uniforms. There were boys in entire suits of black and green velvet, with top boots; men with blue and red uniforms and bright steel helmets, and others in green serge coats and regulation black trousers. The men in costume were, of course, the most popular with the fair ones.

Time was passed pleasantly in dancing, drinking, and seeing the sights. Everybody danced, and most of the men danced well, all with cigars in their mouths and some in their shirt-sleeves. The event of the day was the grand dramatic performance given by a few amateur actors in a wooden open-topped shanty, erected on the grounds. The theatre itself was very simple and convenient, as the audience in front could see behind the scenes and on the stage at the same time, and the stage-manager walked to and fro unconcernedly, but quite unnoticed by the performers. The play was in German, of course; the hero was a shoemaker: Schnapps was the villain, and the plot was, and to the writer continues to be, the mystery. The performance was well received.

At sundown the numerous beer-libations began to have their effect upon some of the gallant pic-nickers. There was considerable

omping and kissing, not exactly *comme il faut*, but no conduct beyond the bounds of decency—noisy singing and violent dancing
and love-making, but not the least viciousness in the gathering.
On the contrary, the utmost good feeling prevailed and everybody
seemed to feel good, as may be shown by one of the incidents of
the day.   The photographer's wife went to see the panorama next
door, charge 5 cents, and when the panorama man passed by, the
photographer offered him that amount in United States currency.
The panorama man would not accept, the photographer insisted.
"Nun, sehen sie her," urged the panorama man, "wir sind alle
beide kunstler." "("Now see here, we are both artists.")

Then there was beer all around for the sentiment.

www.ingramcontent.com/pod-product-compliance
Lightning Source LLC
Chambersburg PA
CBHW022011050726
47499CB00007BA/2319